NADINE LITTLE

We Are Not Angels

The Warrior Angels 1

LITTLE
PUBLISHING

My mailing list members get free books and unique behind-the-scenes material.

Members are always the first to hear about my new books and discounts.

See the back of the book for details on how to join.

'For the angel of death spread his wings on the blast,
and breathed in the face of the foe as he passed;
And the eyes of the sleepers waxed deadly and chill,
and their hearts but once heaved, and forever grew still.'
Lord Byron, *The Destruction of Sennacherib*.

'I'll show you fear in a handful of dust.'
T.S. Eliot

1

I hate the silence more than the screams. Silence means they're hunting.

So much for a hospital being a safe space.

I hunker deeper in the cupboard. A shelf creaks against my spine and bandages rustle in plastic tubs. I slip a couple of crinkling dressing packets into my backpack.

A weight thuds on the other side of the door.

"Please!" a man yelps. "They just rebuilt my leg! I'm no threat to anyone." Footsteps slap-scrape, slap-scrape down the corridor. "I recycle! Please—"

An awful singing drowns the voice, rising in a crescendo past the cupboard door. My gut twists. The man screams once. Then nothing. I suck a gulp of dusty air and hold my breath.

They move so quietly, it's like they're not there.

But they are.

"I'm bedridden, you merciless bastards," quails a woman's voice. "Why don't you take that arrow and stick it up your—"

Singing and silence.

The patients should have been evacuated last week after the shelter in place order was lifted and cities started to empty. Plus, healthy adults are the worst offenders, not the sick, injured and infirm. Why target the weak? But the woman

1

is right.

The angels are merciless.

My fault for lingering here so long but the building is vast. Dawn arrived before I knew it.

I stay in the cupboard until my legs go numb and the light fades beneath the door. A protein bar soothes the grumbles in my stomach. Tiredness weighs my eyelids but I dare not sleep. I sip water from my bottle—single-use plastic.

Guess I'm going to hell, if I'm not already there.

The door squeaks open to a slice of shadowed corridor. Electric lights glow elsewhere in the building, comforting while the rest of the world falls apart.

We probably have a few days, a week at the most, before the services shut down. The benefit of Scotland receiving most of its power from renewable energy. It could be over by then, the survivors crawling from their caves to pick up not quite where we left off. Unsuitably chastised.

I tip-toe along the corridor, my boots hushed on the linoleum. I skirt abandoned hospital beds, their sheets trailing to the floor. Powder cakes the creases. Rot sweetens each breath and coats my tongue.

I was horrified to discover the dead and dying patients when I emerged from hiding yesterday night to scavenge the Western General Hospital, assuming it would be empty. Last week, the police and army tried to evacuate Holyrood and rein in the panicked flight of civilians after the military defences collapsed at the coast and angels entered the UK. We should have known from the speed Europe fell but it all happened so fast. The angels swept into the streets of Edinburgh five days ago and took the castle. The patients must have been abandoned in the chaos.

At least the smell keeps other people away.

I prowl to the kitchen in the bowels of the ground level. Cans clunk into my backpack. I shove in bags of cornflakes, dried rice and pasta. The zip strains over the haul. I eye the huge tins of potatoes, peas and peaches but they're too bulky. It would be a waste to open one, the contents going off quicker than even I can eat them.

My ex-boyfriend always commented on how much I packed away. At first, I thought it was because he paid for dinner. Turned out, it was because he thought a woman should subsist on lettuce leaves and a glass of water.

I wonder if he's gone.

My foot kicks a kidney dish and it skitters along the floor. I wince at the ring of metal and squeeze the carving knife in my sweaty hand. Taken from my own kitchen, the blade is long enough to be classed as a mini-sword.

No one has ever got close enough to use a knife on an angel but it discourages humans from getting a bit excited.

"Is somebody there?" wheezes a voice from a bright archway into a ward.

Should I pretend I'm a ghost and run? What good can I possibly do? I don't even know first aid.

I peek around the edge. The room resembles the aftermath of a blanket explosion. A figure lies in the only bed not shoved away from the wall at a haphazard angle.

"Help me," the man whispers.

A shrivelled bag hangs on the drip stand by his bed. A drainage unit clipped to the side of the frame balloons with yellow fluid. The man's head slumps on the pillow, haloed by tufts of brown hair. His eyes are sunken, too bright, his skin tight to his bones. The stench of sickness and waste slaps me in the face.

"I'm sorry," I say. "I'm not a doctor."

"Take me with you."

His sheets stick to where one leg ends above the knee, stained pink and yellow-green.

Was he injured in the initial panic or the massacre that followed?

I swallow hard and force myself closer, slipping my knife into my belt and shrugging off my backpack.

"Here," I say. "Drink slowly."

He snatches the bottle in one clawed hand. Plastic crumples. A fountain of water splashes onto his hospital gown. He guzzles the liquid and chokes.

I pluck the bottle from his weak grip. *"Slowly."*

Is it cruel to prolong the inevitable? Maybe I should take a pillow and put it over his face.

He slurps another mouthful, splashing more as his hands shake. I build a pyramid of jelly pots and protein bars on the wheeled table beside his bed, adding an unopened bottle of water.

"Take me with you," he says.

His chest rattles when he breathes.

"I'm sorry. I can't."

"Take me with you!"

He lunges for me and the bottle hits the floor, spraying water on my boots and jeans. His arm clips the table, catapulting food across the room. I stumble out of reach. The man howls the same words, over and over.

"I'm sorry," I say but he doesn't seem to hear.

Spittle foams around his mouth, his lips twisted in a snarl. He flails at me, though I put an empty bed between us and inch towards the door. A jelly pot squishes under my heel. Strawberry mixes with the scent of piss and death.

I sprint from the hospital and don't look back.

2

Two Weeks Ago

"Does this mean we're going to hell since we didn't believe?"

My best friend and neighbour from across the landing sits in her wheelchair sandwiched between my patchwork couch and a bookshelf. She usually walks with a cane so it's obviously been a bad day for her pain-wise.

"I'm watching it and still don't believe it," I say, staring at my mega TV tuned to BBC News. The only extravagant thing in my flat. My second-hand PlayStation sits underneath in a coil of wires.

I haven't gamed in days.

"You'll probably be all right, Maia, but I've got two strikes against me." She flips a curl of pink hair over her shoulder. Her skirt is a froth of rainbow lace, her white boots knee-high.

"Oh, come on, Steph," I say. "I understand the trans thing but, as far as I know, God doesn't hate the differently abled."

"Maybe not. But look at them and tell me they don't make you a little insecure about who gets into heaven."

On the TV, the image cuts from the presenter in a studio to a camera panning the live scenes direct from Rome. The subjects of the news report stand on the Colonnades between the statues of the saints and look down on the people stuffed into St. Peter's Square. The shot cuts to a close up—tall, muscled, perfect cheekbones and skin. The females have shoulders as broad as the males, their modesty covered with robes. White-gold wings sparkle in the sunlight as if the feathers are fringed with precious metal. Other figures have wings of turquoise, amethyst or emerald. They appeared in the sky above the Vatican two days ago, triggering a religious fervour bordering on insanity.

Angels.

"We don't even know if they're real," I say.

Steph quirks an eyebrow at me.

"Fine. We don't know if they're actually from heaven or prove the existence of God or whatever."

Steph nods at the screen. *"They* believe."

A reporter with a finger to her ear and a puff of a microphone stands on the other side of a metal barrier separating the crowd from the media. Her voice is almost drowned out by the screaming people in St. Peter's Square waving at the angels on the Colonnades, begging for their attention, their faces flushed despite the crisp November day. They clutch rosaries, crucifixes and statues of the Virgin Mary. Several kneel in prayer, jostled and tripped over by the semi-hysterical crowd.

"Of course they believe. Now they can shove how right they were in everybody's face." It comes out more vehemently than I intended.

"That sounds personal," Steph says, dragging her gaze from the TV. "Your family? You never talk about them."

"My mum died when I was eleven."

"I'm sorry."

I shrug. "She kept my father in check but after she died, he went all-out religious—church, confession, nightly prayers. God forbid I wear anything but thick wool skirts below the knee and shapeless jumpers. Of course, I started my period after my mum was gone. That was a horror show of sermons on how women are unclean and full of sin."

"Jesus."

"Yeah, don't say that in his earshot or he'll lecture you for three hours."

"When did you last see him?"

Another shrug. "Ten years ago. He must be loving this."

The camera cuts from the reporter to the chanting and howling crowd in St. Peter's then the angels watching impassively. Their chiselled faces resemble the statues they stand beside. Next is the empty Papal Station in front of the basilica, awaiting the Pope and an angel to address the world.

Just thinking it sounds weird.

My phone buzzes on the couch cushion. An unfamiliar number.

The networks have been patchy with everyone and their mother calling each other to ask, "Are you seeing this? ARE YOU SEEING THIS?"

I scoop it up and press the button. "Hello?"

"Now is the time to repent, Mary, before it's too late."

A spasm runs through me and I almost lob my phone through the window. Just his voice is enough to awaken the familiar shame. It took me years to get rid of the guilt his religion drowns in.

"My name is Maia," I say. "Is that all you called to tell me, John?"

I changed my name and moved out of my father's house as

soon as I turned sixteen. Maia means 'brave warrior'. She's also the earth goddess of spring, my favourite time of year.

"Plead confession with the Holy Angels and wash yourself free of sin, Mary," he says over the faint click of his rosary.

He called me his virgin Mary (gross) and mapped out my life—marriage to a god-fearing man, then kids. I would be a devout Catholic woman. I just wanted to crawl in the mud and climb trees with the local boys. The day they let me play on their games consoles, I fell in love.

"I'm surprised you're not at the Vatican with the screaming masses," I say, and ignore the little jab of guilt at my pettiness.

"I don't need to be present to feel God's love. I'm blessed simply to bear witness to this miracle."

"Is there anything else you want to say? Maybe ask how I'm doing?"

"Come and pray with me, Mary. Families should be together during this momentous occasion. I'd like to introduce you to a gentleman from my church. He'd make a fine provider—"

"Goodbye, John." I jab the phone and toss it on the coffee table.

My hands are shaking. How the hell did he get my number?

Steph squeezes my arm. "You okay?"

I shake my head. "Speak of the bloody devil—just your typical call from dear old Dad. It's like no time has passed."

We watch the people mill about St. Peter's Square, the angels on the Colonnades unmoved. A jerky camera shot shows one stretching his wings, the span at least six metres, and the crowd, "Ooh," in appreciation.

"Families really suck, don't they?" Steph says, softly, her eyes back on the screen. "Mine dropped me quicker than you can say gender reassignment surgery."

"The term is a long one, it can't have been that quick." I flash her a grin.

She sticks out her tongue. "Smart arse."

The news presenter babbles her voiceover while the cameras pan the crowd, the angels, the basilica.

"Wait, something's happening." I sit forward.

The mob of people on the TV falls silent. Doves wheel around the basilica, released earlier by some nutter in the crush. Because white represents purity and blah blah blah.

The reporter, still with her finger in her ear, whispers into her microphone and the camera cuts to the Pope exiting St. Peter's, the hem of his vestments sweeping the stone. His staff clicks in the quiet, topped by a crucifix.

I hate that I remember the names for everything—mitre, Papal ferula, pallium.

An angel strides behind the Pope, the tips of her golden wings almost brushing the floor, like his robes. Crimson hair tumbles to her ankles.

There was some uproar that the angel representative was female. It made me despise religion all over again.

The Pope and the angel take a seat at the Papal Station. The Pope addresses the gathered worshippers in Italian, the reporter on her voiceover too excited to translate. The Pope nods to the angel. She leans towards the microphone. I hold my breath.

"I can't believe we're going to hear her speak," Steph says. "Do you think she knows English? What does the voice of an angel even sound like?"

"If you shut up for a minute, maybe we'll find out."

Steph mimes sealing her lips and wheels her chair closer to the TV.

10

The angel sweeps her bright-blue eyes over the crowd and raises her head to her brethren gathered on the Colonnades.

"We are the Protectorate," she says in a voice that is deeper, harsher, than I expected. "It is our duty to protect the universes."

I raise my brows at Steph. "Universes?"

She shushes me with a wave of her hand.

"We allowed you time to reverse the damage you have done," the female angel continues, the only sound the clap of doves' wings. "We had hoped for your sake you would but you have waited too long. Remember this day, humans, those of you who survive. This is your reckoning."

The angels ringing the Colonnades throw open their robes. Each holds a slim, black bow. Arrows fly into the crowd.

The crimson-haired angel swivels in her seat and stabs the sapphire tip of an arrow into the Pope's eye.

3

I run until the streets and the night obscure the hospital. The tins jink in my backpack and drum on my spine. The roads are empty of people, everything hushed and frosted with ice. I hitch a left off of Crewe Road South past a Bank of Scotland and burned-out cars onto Comely Bank, my boots slipping and forcing me to slow.

I should have left Edinburgh when the evacuation began and every sane person fled. The angels focus on populated areas so there's more chance of avoiding them in the countryside. I'd wanted to stay with Steph as long as possible but I left it too late. As soon as I decided to move, the angels arrived, forcing me to hide instead of escaping the city. I waited four days then emerged from my temporary shelter to scavenge the hospital, only to come within a feather's breadth of angels almost immediately. The Western General isn't that far from my flat in Martello Court, either—thirty minutes' walk.

I liked feeling close to Steph.

I jog past a Waitrose, the windows broken. Streetlights reflect on shards of glass. Candles flicker in several of the townhouses opposite.

How many people huddle inside? I'm a little jealous if their central heating still works.

Shadows glide around the corner of a Boots chemist, the sign flickering blue and white. Something crunches under a shoe. My heart skips but no wings sprout from shoulder blades.

Death doesn't come in the night, slinking in the shadows in a robe of black. Death stalks in daylight with the whisper of wings and the song of an arrow.

"Where you goin' in such a hurry, eh?"

A boy steps into my path, a dark bandana cinching a clod of greasy hair. A second boy slides into place beside him. His grin is the only thing I can see beyond the pit of his hoodie.

"Nowhere special," I say.

"That's a braw bag you've got there," a girl says behind me. "What's in it?"

Two girls range across the pavement, blocking my exit. A parked car obstructs my path to the road. I shift to keep the four teenagers in sight and put my back to the wall. The girl who spoke has a shaved head and black streaks of make-up smeared under her eyes. The second girl tries to look menacing while shivering in a cropped denim jacket.

"Food, water," I say. "Some bandages."

"Hand it ower," the first boy says.

"Find your own."

A penknife clicks open. "Hand it ower or we cut ye."

I scan their young, dirt-smeared faces. None of them are over fifteen. Are their parents gone?

"We shouldn't fight each other. Now is the time to band together."

It's not the most rousing speech, and a bit of a lie. The last thing I want to do is join a bunch of feral teenagers. But the sentiment is real.

"It's survival o' the fittest and you're outnumbered. Gie us the bag and we let ye go."

Three Stanley knives glint in the bronze of a streetlight. The teenagers' hands are filthy, dirt half-mooned in their fingernails. The shivering girl is at risk of cutting herself, never mind anybody else.

I sigh. "Do I have to *Crocodile Dundee* your asses?"

A puzzled glance flicks between the group.

"Wit the fuck ye talking 'bout, eh?" says their bandana-ed leader.

Bloody zoomers.

I draw the carving knife from my belt, nice and slow. Eyes widen. The grin vanishes from the oval of the hoodie.

"I'll cut you before you get anywhere near me so I suggest you all bugger off home to your mummies," I say.

The bandana kid spits on the concrete. I wave my blade in a threatening half-circle. They edge away to put the car between us.

"I hope ye get dusted," the shaven-headed girl snarls.

The teenagers lope into Fettes Avenue towards the high school. I wait for the slap of their trainers to fade. Cold nips at my fingers and the tip of my nose. I hustle down the road, pausing every few hundred metres to listen for pursuit. A van burns outside the Domino's in Stockbridge. I warm my hands near the flames and imagine taking a bite of chicken and mushroom pizza, the cheese hot enough to scald the roof of my mouth. My stomach rumbles despite the protein bar.

I need to find a base with working gas and electricity where I can hole up and wait, all cosy and quiet. Rural or semi-rural. Get a camping stove and torches for when the services quit. Plenty of books so I don't get bored.

Apocalypse? Piece of cake.

I creep north-east towards Leith and the main A199 road on the outskirts of Edinburgh, knife out to discourage other enterprising neds. Warehouses and businesses replace the residential streets, the lights dimmer and further apart. The sea laps softly beyond the buildings. The night settles around me. No clouds mar the sky, the stars twinkling like chips of ice. A sliver of moon gilds the edges of the world silver.

At Harry Lauder Road, a snarl of crashed and abandoned cars blocks the junction, smelling of spilled petrol mixed with the sweetness of anti-freeze. I weave around the cold metal and continue south through Portobello to the A1. The road looks more like a car park than a major thoroughfare, the blackened skeletons of vehicles eerie in the light of the moon. At least it's too dark to notice the dust that no doubt speckles the tarmac.

A truck looms out of the night, skewed across the road through the flimsy central reservation. My breath fogs the glass as I peer into the cab then climb inside. It stinks of stale oil and trucker sweat. There's a bed in the rear that isn't too stained. I pull the curtains over the windows and lock the doors, the key still in the ignition.

The driver must have left in a hurry or his dust has mingled with the dirt in the footwell.

My shivering exploration by the light of the dashboard finds a portable heater tucked under the bed. I happily plug it into the twelve-volt socket and switch it on. The small space soon warms and sucks the chill from the sheets.

How many people will die from the cold before the angels find them? Will their deaths count?

From what I know of the merciless bastards, I doubt it.

I cuddle into the bed and try to sleep, lulled by the call of a tawny owl somewhere in the dark.

4

Five Days Ago

"Are you sure you won't come with me?" I say.

"Be serious, Maia. I'll just slow you down."

"I don't care about that."

Steph leans half on her door frame and half on her cane. Diamonds sparkle from the handle to the shaft in the flickering lights of the landing between our flats.

We bedazzled the walking stick one Saturday afternoon, tipsy on wine and giggling like idiots. I was sober enough to stop us short of vajazzling. No one needs glitter there.

The jewel theme continues to Steph's tight, white jeans and top. Her wig is sunflower-yellow today.

"You saw what happened when the army fought those things at the border," Steph says. "We can't kill them."

"We don't have to kill them. We just need to wait it out where they won't come hunting. Like the world's biggest game of hide and seek."

Steph waves her hand at the scuffed linoleum, beige walls and dented metal door to the stairwell. "What better place than here? You've given me enough supplies to last a few weeks. It could be done by then."

"Listen to the downstairs neighbours weeping and carrying on. It's like they've invited everyone round for an end of days party. The noise might attract attention. The angels are getting closer to Edinburgh every day."

"Then I'll be very, *very* quiet."

I jiggle the backpack on my shoulders, the weight already uncomfortable. Maybe I shouldn't have packed so many books but paranormal romance is my second love after gaming and it's not like I can take my PlayStation.

My first boyfriend ridiculed my reading material and hated that I could beat him at FIFA. He didn't realise that romance doesn't make you a weakling—it makes you a warrior strong enough to capture the hearts of monsters.

"It's safer to stay away from people," I say.

"Maia, that was true even before the angels started hunting us."

We share a grim fist bump.

"Promise me you'll be careful. Keep your curtains closed. Don't use too many lights. Stay out of sight."

She folds me in a hug since she's miles taller. She smells of Parma Violets and jasmine.

"I promise, Maia. We'll have cocktails to celebrate when this is over."

"Deal."

I turn to go and she grabs my arm.

"Promise *me* you won't fight them. I've seen the stuff you play—all that dystopian hero shit. One man against the bad guys. This is real life, not a computer game."

"I don't plan on fighting, though it would be nice to find something that hurts them."

But nothing worked.

After the massacre at the Vatican—though it's hard to call it a massacre when it left no bodies—thousands of angels appeared in Italy then spread across the world. Armies retaliated. Cities became warzones. Bullets seemed to bounce off the angels or pass right through, their reaction no more than an annoyed flick of wings. They walked unscathed from craters of flame, sparks dancing between their feathers. There were rumours of casualties under heavy fire—bodies torn yet strangely bloodless—but no one survived long enough to verify. No one got close. Arrows sang through the sky. President Weston irradiated half of America to no avail. Our First Minister showed a little restraint but Scotland is still more cratery than it used to be.

Steph's manicured nails pinch my bicep. "Nothing hurts them. That's kinda what invincible means."

"Everything has a weakness, otherwise it wouldn't be fair."

"You poor, sweet romantic." She envelops me in another hug. "Take care of yourself, Maia. I never thought I'd find a friend in this shitty block of flats so I want you here again when the angels fuck off back to wherever they came from. If they even do what they said and don't slaughter us all."

I shudder. They'd better honour their word. The only reason I'm still functioning is because this nightmare has an end point.

"I just wish we could make their job harder," I say. "Give them a real battle."

"And have them around longer? No, thanks. Like you said—we don't need to kill them, we just need to hide. So, go. *Hide*. I'll be fine."

She kisses my temple and shoves me gently away. I wait to hear the clunk of her locks and the scrape of her security chain.

Maybe she's the smart one, battening the hatches at home where things are comfortable and familiar. We could have spent the apocalypse eating snacks and playing *Call of Duty*. There'll still be people online, desperate to keep going until the electricity runs out and their lives end. Steph and I could amuse ourselves with board games when the power quits.

I pause on the steps and glance back at our doors facing each other across the landing. Part of me aches to stay but there's an itch under my skin screaming at me to run. Martello Court is the tallest block of flats in Edinburgh.

A beacon for creatures with wings.

Music and wailing drift from the landing of the next floor down. I shake my head and trot the six storeys to basement level. The underground garage is a cold concrete box, diesel fumes leached into the brick. I stroke my fingers along the bright-red bonnet of my Mitsubishi L200 Warrior.

So I have one other extravagance. She makes me feel huge and unstoppable. I love using the handle to haul myself inside. We could go anywhere.

But she'd draw too much attention, especially with the angels closing in. Who knows how far away they are now? There were sightings in Glasgow only yesterday.

I give my Mitsubishi a pat and leave her in the gloom of the garage.

Okay, my car could've been more fuel-efficient. A hybrid or something. I could've walked ten minutes to the shops instead of driving. Multiple times. I could've been vegan, except I like steak, and bacon rolls. I should've recycled instead of shoving everything into a bin bag since it was easier than separating it. My flat is tiny so I don't have space for boxes of cardboard, plastic and glass. It's simple to point fingers and fire arrows.

It's not simple to change.

Though I bet this is not what the Scottish Parliament pictured when they declared a climate emergency.

Skirting a blockage of abandoned vehicles, I disappear into the streets of Edinburgh.

5

The pleading voices reach me as soon as I leave the hulk of the lorry behind, the battery flat. Frost rimes the inside of the windscreen. I thought about hiding there until dark but it's too damn cold.

Seems the people ahead made the same wrong choice.

Steam wisps into the air from a crumpled bonnet, the red Ford Focus nose-first in the metal crash barrier. A man and woman scramble away from a figure in the middle of the road, the woman clutching a baby carrier to her chest. Two arrows sing and the carrier clatters to the tarmac. A shriek emanates from the covered basket, little hands and feet waving free from the swaddling. The angel kneels in the road. Beautiful golden wings arch from her shoulders. She tucks a curl of crimson hair behind her ear.

The angel from the Vatican.

What the hell is she doing over here? Have they dusted the whole of Italy? Is there anyone left in Europe?

The angel cradles the baby in her arms, her face a picture of blue-eyed serenity.

She slides an arrow into the tiny chest.

The swaddling deflates. The little arms and legs crumble. A desolate cry echoes over the frozen landscape of cars and concrete and cold blue sky.

Apparently, the dust of murdered people is rich in nutrients and minerals to encourage plant growth. It also detoxifies the air and soil. Better than leaving a mess of rotten corpses.

As if we should thank them.

The angels were quite vocal once they figured out how to use our media sources to communicate, though it was always a different one for each broadcast, as if they couldn't decide on a single spokesperson. They said every death tallied protects our planet's future. The universes' future. We deserved it for abusing our home.

The righteousness really pissed me off.

The angel spreads her glorious wings and launches into the sky. The wind of her flight stirs the three small dust piles powdering the road. I wait for the heavy beats to fade. My breath puffs white. I scramble to the scrub on the other side of the carriageway and use it for cover to head south-east in the opposite direction.

It takes an hour to reach the City Bypass. Depressed by the multi-vehicle pile-ups, I cut back on myself and walk north off the main roads into Musselburgh, foraging in shops along the way. Broken glass crunches on the floor. Soot stains the walls with the acrid stench of fire. I shake dust from an abandoned holdall and empty the contents—a man's clothes. I keep a grey hoodie, t-shirt, black shirt and some toothpaste. A Co-Op has barely been touched. My boots leave prints in the dust. I swallow the revulsion and tip-toe down the aisles, breathing softly through my nose. I swipe tins, sweets, tea bags and dried milk. The bag fills with toilet roll, lighters, candles and batteries. Not great for the environment but I select biodegradable moist wipes to atone.

Residential streets end in a strip of woodland surrounding an industrial estate. I'm out of breath by the time I drag my bulging holdall and backpack across.

I need to get indoors before my luck runs out and I stumble on a hunting party. The name of the next store disagrees: Go Outdoors.

"Sweet," I whisper, trotting towards the entrance, which glides open.

I partake in an enthusiastic game of *Supermarket Sweep*, camping-style and without the trolley, then heave my haul up the road to a roundabout, wincing at the straps digging into my arms, shoulder and back. Straight ahead, two archways flank the entrance to some kind of driveway. The sign reads 'National Trust for Scotland' and 'Newhailes'.

A country estate? I think I've found my hidey-hole.

I stagger down the driveway into a tunnel of woodland, my multitude of bags crushing my bones with the weight, my legs wobbly but desperate to run.

It's not safe to travel in daylight.

The road splits and I swing right, ducking under a chain past two stone gatepiers. The driveway curves in an oval forecourt in front of a huge Palladian house surrounded by bare trees. Mullioned windows watch beneath a central, hipped roof as I pant over the flattened gravel and scan the sky. A double staircase leads to an upper door. A second, shabbier door sits in the gloom formed under the archway of the stairs.

I twist the iron ring of the lower entrance but the wood sticks. Slamming my shoulder into it twice tumbles me into a musty servants' entrance. The door wedges shut and I drag a bookcase in front of it. I leave my goodies and explore.

The ground floor contains a kitchen and a maze of narrow

corridors, probably so the staff could move unseen, dusting and polishing without offending the eyeballs of their masters. An equally narrow and rickety staircase leads to the first floor. The entrance is grand, though the front door—reached by the double staircase outside—is worn. I try the handle but it appears to be locked.

A painting of a kissing couple hangs above an elaborate rococo fireplace, the lovers flanked by snow and winter-bare leaves. The rest of the paintings in the sprawling villa feature men in powdered wigs and red coats. The place smells of mothballs and dust.

Normal dust.

I hop up the steps to the second floor, the iron banister crafted into a circular pattern. Every bedroom, and there are many, has a four-poster bed of heavy brocade. Every room has a fireplace and a painting. My reflection gives me a scare in the mirrored dining room. I hold my breath in the library to keep from disintegrating the fragile books packed on the shelves. A mounted sword in a glass case is fixed to the wall on either side of the obligatory painting above the fireplace. I drag a chair of cracked leather over the carpet, open a glass box and lift a sword from the hooks.

Hefty.

The blade scrapes and rings faintly when I draw it from the scabbard. Dull grey tapers to a sharp point, the pommel swelling into a bud shape. The handle is ridged and solid in my hand. Rust flecks and pits the blade. Iron or steel? Would an iron-age weapon survive this long? It looks ancient, whatever the provenance. I step off the chair and try a few practice swings. The sword whistles through the air.

Way scarier than my carving knife.

I fix the scabbard to my belt and finish my exploration with the sword in my hand. I may stab an invisible enemy and cry, "Begone foul beast," a few times. Imagine myself as the heroine, dazzling the monsters with her battle prowess and melting even the coldest of hearts.

Okay, maybe I *am* too much of a romantic. More slaughter, less love—that's what this world needs until the angels bugger off.

The rear of the house opens into a conservatory with a view of the Forth beyond a long, untidy lawn and a block of woodland. The lights still flash on the bridges where they rise above the trees. In the heart of the house, I find a windowless security room, one wall a bank of screens above a control desk faced by a chair on wheels. The monitors switch on at the press of a button and blue-grey light fills the space, the cameras showing the grand entrance, the library, dining room, several bedrooms, corridors and the conservatory, plus the forecourt, all empty.

A perfect place to wait out the apocalypse.

6

I miss the sounds of people, even the stupid kid who ran constantly back and forth in the flat above mine. I miss the comforting thud of his feet, the murmur of voices, the tinny blare of a TV. Steph laughing at something stupid I've said. Now, there's only silence. But at least it's not the silence of hunting angels. I don't see a single one on any of the security cameras.

I build my nest beneath the control panel—inflatable mattress, sleeping bag, blankets. It would be too creepy to sleep in a bedroom and risk waking in the dead of night to a figure looming over the bed, wings or no. It's cosy in my little cave since the door locks from the inside and there's a heater. It'll be cold when the electricity fails but I have candles and a portable stove.

The internet eases the loneliness. I huddle over the blue glow of my phone, reading tales of survival, defiance, loss but no success in finding a weapon to hurt the angels. The access is patchy—some servers are still operational while others have crashed or their vulnerable power source has been lost. Twitter works, though there's no Facebook, WhatsApp or Instagram. Military web pages and government information sites are available but haven't been updated in the last few days. I text

Steph and she's doing okay. Worrying about what will happen if her pain meds run out. I treasure the contact. Will it end soon, too? If Scotland's servers use renewable energy, the internet may keep going until there's a fault in the system, with no engineers available for repairs since the whole of humanity is in hiding, however much is left of it. The problem will be accessing the internet when my phone battery dies and the main grid goes down.

I watch the security screens during the day and patrol the house at night, my hand cupped around the beam of a torch, my heart flapping against my ribs. The lights work but I leave them off. The bulbs in the servants' corridors stay on as I can't find the switches. It doesn't seem to matter since there are barely any windows down there.

I carry the sword everywhere.

I raid a nearby library and stuff my bags with books, games and DVDs after I find a portable player that runs on electricity or a lithium battery. I borrow Bear Grylls' *How to Stay Alive*. It says it's the ultimate survival guide for any situation and, while it doesn't specifically mention angels of death, it has some interesting information. Inspired, I set snares in the woodland surrounding the house. I'm not too disappointed when they don't catch anything as I can't imagine myself gutting and skinning a rabbit.

Sorry, Mr Grylls.

I watch movies, read and play *Solitaire* in my solitary room. My meals consist mostly of pasta, cereal and tinned fruit. I swiped some vitamin pills so hopefully that staves off the scurvy. Every morning, I brew a cup of tea in the kitchen and drink it in the conservatory, watching the mist fade over the grass and the bridge lights flicker on the Forth.

It's peaceful, slightly boring, but not a bad way to survive.

* * *

My boots pound on the thin carpet of the corridor. Grey daylight halos doorways. I jog circuits around the library wing since the corridor has few windows. The sword bounces against my thigh, my breath rasping, my muscles warm. I stretch to cool down and head to the kitchen to fill a glass with water, sniffing and taking an experimental sip. Tastes and smells like water.

Most of Scotland's water is gravity-fed from reservoirs so the supply should stay fresh as long as the treatment works run and no pipes burst.

The cold liquid curls in my belly and I swipe the beaded glass on my forehead. Dreaming of a tepid bath in a metal tub that's older than me, I hop up the rickety servants' steps into the grand entrance.

Rain patters through the open door.

An angel examines the painting above the fireplace, his head cocked. Huge, black wings are tucked against his back. My glass shatters on the tile. The angel pivots smoothly and raises his bow.

I imagined this moment. What I would say—something kick-ass and defiant. Cool in the face of terror.

I yelp, "Oh, bugger off, you feathery bastard," and throw myself backwards.

An arrow sings and embeds in the wall near my head, close enough to feel the horrible, pulsing draw of it. The dark shaft swirls a nauseating blue.

Would touching the thing be enough to dust me?

I scrabble away and fall down the steps into the servants' corridors. Wings rustle behind me.

At least he can't fly and attack me from above, only bury an arrow in my back.

I dodge and duck and try not to vomit. Arrows sing, thunking into the wall, the roof, the floor. My gut twists at the wail of each one, anticipating a sharp pain, a sucking horror.

Then nothing.

My muscles wobble from my earlier, much gentler, run. I pant on musty air, bounce off walls and heave myself around corners. I can't hear the angel beyond the hammer of my heart but I know he's there. I waste a few precious seconds hopping from foot to foot at the servants' entrance, wedged shut and blocked by the bookcase.

Are there more angels outside? If I get the barrier free in time, will I blunder into a hail of arrows?

I dive into another corridor. It twists into a long, straight passage leading to the kitchen. The angel steps around the corner and blocks my path.

When did the bastard back-track?

I skid to a halt. All my air rushes out in a whoosh.

"Running is futile," he says, his voice soft and precise.

"Screw you," I squeak.

He's tall. Broad shoulders, narrow hips. He's a slice of darkness in the dim corridor from his black wings and hair to his dark eyes and black, laced boots, the laces continuing up his trousers. The hems of his long-sleeved top flop over his hands. It's loose at the neck and black, like the rest of his clothes, held open by more laces to show a slab of chest.

If they'd all looked like this, maybe we wouldn't have been fooled so easily. He's more fallen angel than heaven-sent.

He loops the wicked bow across his shoulder.

"Out of arrows?" I say, a quaver ruining my mocking tone. "What a pity."

He draws a sword as long as my whole body from a sheath on his spine. The metal glows eerie blue and my stomach dives to my toes. I fumble for the blade at my waist. It takes two tries to free the weapon. I point it at him and the tip jumps in time to my pulse. Rust speckles the carpet.

The angel smirks. "Are you trained in swordplay?"

I slide my feet apart and angle my shoulders to copy his stance. Shame I can't copy his expression of perfect arrogance—my eyes are wide and I'm pretty sure I'm biting my lip.

"I've watched movies," I say. "Best training there is."

I grip my sword in two hands and raise it to eyeball level like I'm Beatrix Kiddo in *Kill Bill*.

The angel's eyes glitter. "I doubt it."

He twirls a fancy pattern in the air, the tip of the blade grazing the ceiling and returning to wink at my face. Coldness wafts from the sword and goosepimples my arms.

"Then you're going to be really embarrassed when I beat you," I say.

"You are human. You cannot beat me."

I bare my teeth but it's more grimace than snarl. "Prove it."

What am I doing, goading an angel? I'm going to die.

His blade thrusts for my face. I shriek and slap it with my sword, sending them both into the wall where they slice the paper. Metal scrapes on metal. He forces me back, jabbing for my neck, my torso, my legs while I clumsily parry and try not to trip on my own feet. His wings fill the corridor and whisper on the walls. He swings for a forehead-cleaving blow, and metal rings. The impact screams through my arms and down my spine.

He's too strong. If we were outside, unencumbered by the narrow space, I'd already be a pile of twitching limbs.

Then dust.

He hacks at my head. I need both arms to block and the effort trembles in my muscles, my palms slick on the hilt of my sword. Rust patters my face. A knife appears in the angel's free hand while I strain to keep his sword from embedding in my skull. It streaks towards me with a flick of his wrist. A burning line carves my ribs.

"No!" I gasp and stumble back, metal rasping as our swords slide clear.

I clap a hand to my side and my fingers come away red. Not too much.

But enough.

The rest of my blood drains from my face.

Will it hurt? Will I watch myself dissolve? I don't want to die.

A tear scalds my cheek. The angel cocks his head, cold and dispassionate while I swoon against the wall and wait to become one of the dusted.

And wait.

"We also use human weapons," the angel says.

I glance at my feet. Wiggle my toes. Still there, not clods of powder.

"Oh," I say.

The angel's sword sings through the air. I squeal and dive off the wall. Our blades ring. My arms weaken. Pain sizzles between my temples, sickness cramping my gut at the proximity of the blue, glowing sword. The clang of metal drives spikes of noise into my eardrums.

The angel tosses another knife. I ram my shoulder into the wall to avoid it and the blade tugs at my sleeve. The angel's sword drops closer, my arms shaking under the strength of his one-armed assault.

"How many knives—do you have—you bastard?" I pant, and duck away.

He swings, his sword gripped in both fists. The killing blow. My puny muscles will buckle and I'll help him by slicing off my own face before his blade sinks into my forehead.

His sword tip catches the ceiling.

Instead of seizing the moment to scamper away like a sensible person, I lunge forward, cursing myself for an idiot.

It won't do anything. My weapon will glance off his side like all the bullets that came before. He'll smirk, free his blade and lop off my head.

Angels are invincible.

So I'm somewhat surprised when my sword slides neatly between his ribs.

7

Force of habit has me almost squeaking, "I'm sorry!" to the angel skewered on the end of my blade.

We British are nothing if not polite.

The angel drops to his knees. His sword clatters to the threadbare carpet and I flinch away from the sickening pull of the metal. He touches his fingers to the rent in his shirt and stares at the slick of silver.

"So you *can* bleed," I whisper, a little awed myself.

I hurt him. I actually *hurt* him.

He sucks in air and it makes a horrible slurping sound.

Whoops. I really hurt him.

I mean *good*.

Silver stains his shirt and froths around the tear in the material, turning a milky yellow. He looks at the wound, something like panic flitting across his face. I touch my blade to his throat. More milky froth covers the tip.

What the hell? Is the metal *dissolving*? What is his blood made of, acid?

The angel raises his head from the fascination of his injury. Dark eyes meet mine and a jolt shivers down my spine.

"How many more knives do you have?" I say.

One arm hangs at his side, the other hand held out, as if

offering me his blood.

"Six," he says between bubbling breaths.

I glance at his black clothes, tight to his shoulders, flat across his stomach and moulded to his thighs.

"Where?" I say then shake myself. "Don't answer that. Put your hands on your head."

He touches his wound and more blood slicks his fingertips. "Why is it not sealing?"

"What?" I say.

"It should not still be bleeding."

"You mean your blood can clot that fast?"

He heaves a laboured breath. "Why can I not breathe?"

"Uh... a sword in the lung will do that."

He starts to shake his head. My blade slips deeper into his throat. A bead of silver trickles down his neck, skirts his collarbone and pools in the hollow between. More froth nibbles the metal of my sword.

What is this magical weapon made from, steel? Is it the iron or rust reacting to his blood, like metal dissolving in acid? I *knew* every monster had to have a weakness.

Even angels.

"I have been stabbed before," he says. "It seals. It always seals. It does not stop me fighting."

Who got close enough to stab him before? They must have died or the news would have spread across what remains of the internet.

"So this super-sealing or clotting or whatever—that's why our bullets had no effect? You can take all that damage and just keep ticking?"

He lifts his dark gaze to me and my stomach swoops.

"Do you have a name?" I say into his silence, my blade as

34

steady as my voice. When he just looks at me I say, "You know…
what they call you. What do you answer to?"

His ribs spasm on each breath. A rattle starts deep in his
chest and a silver stain sticks his shirt to his side.

If he were mortal, he'd be dead.

"Hunter," he says.

"Hunter the human hunter. Wonderful. Are your best
friends Assassin and Killer?"

"What are best friends?"

I frown at him. "Put your hands on your head, Hunter."

He finally obeys. Silver blood glimmers, thick and glistening
under the dim lights. His shoulders rise and fall heavily.
Despite his wound, his expression settles on arrogant and
smugly righteous.

It pisses me off.

"You could have helped us instead of trying to wipe out half
the population," I say. "Some of us fought to save the planet."

Okay, not me with my petrol-guzzling car and my lazy
recycling but he doesn't need to know that. And I've recently
seen the error of my ways.

"We were built for war, not aid."

I'm assuming he meant to growl but it comes out a wheeze.

"What do you mean, built?"

"Built. Created. Not born."

"Oh, great—Frankenstein's angels."

"We are not angels."

"Clearly not."

I touch my blade to his chin and force it higher. He struggles
to breathe, his hands clasped on his head.

"Have any of you ever died before?"

He swallows and I feel it through the sword. Uncertainty

flickers in his dark—black?—eyes, gone between one blink and the next.

"No," he says.

"Doesn't feel great, does it?"

Another swallow. Another blink.

"No," he says.

We stare at each other, only the bubbling-suck of his breaths filling the corridor. The weight of the sword drags at my hand and aches in my arm. Hunter's great, black wings flare behind him, curling protectively.

What would happen if I drove the blade through his skull? Would he puff into dust or would I have the rotting corpse of an angel to dispose of?

I dreamed of this moment—finding the weapon, becoming a hero. I'd stand on a pile of their pretty bodies and people would chant my name, golden feathers stuck to my skin.

I have one, here, on his knees, bloodied by my blade.

And I can't do it.

Killing is easy on my PlayStation. Not so much in real life.

I retreat a couple of steps. Hunter's eyes widen before his face returns to arrogant.

"It's called mercy, Hunter," I say. "Remember it."

I tug my phone from my pocket and record ten seconds of shaky video. An angel on his knees. Bleeding.

A miracle.

I shuffle backwards, tensed for him to throw another of his hidden knives.

"Wait," he says, his voice strained. "What is your name?"

I pause at the corner of the passageway. He seems smaller, almost vulnerable, his hair flopping into his eyes. His sword lies forgotten on the carpet. His blood dries on the tip of mine in a cloud of froth.

"Maia," I say, and sprint for the servants' entrance.

I yank the bookcase clear but stop with my hand on the metal ring.

What if there *are* more out there, waiting for Hunter to finish his sweep?

I weave through the servants' corridors, avoiding where I left Hunter, and reach the rear door. My blade hacks at the jamb until the swollen wood pops free. The unkempt lawn stretches to the trees. Wind howls around the side of the house, bringing sheets of sleety rain.

Not exactly ideal when my jacket and food are all upstairs.

I leave the door ajar.

They'll expect me to flee. Expect me to run as far and fast as possible instead of staying in the house. Maybe I can trick them into leaving.

Why am I trying to second-guess the monsters? Their minds are as alien as they are.

I barricade myself in the security room, comforted by the glow of the screens. Hunter stumbles into view and leans against a wall, his hand pressed to his side. He takes a couple of deep breaths and I'm glad I can't hear the rattle. He straightens his shoulders and strides for the main entrance. The door swings in the wind. A group of five push inside, led by the statuesque, crimson-haired beauty who stabbed the Pope and the baby as if she were doing no more than skewering a potato.

Her face is hard, sharp. Merciless. She sneers at Hunter and punches him in the jaw.

Not exactly, "Are you all right?"

He sprawls in a tangle of limbs and feathers. She stands over him, yelling. She definitely wants to kick him. She addresses the rest of the group and they dive outside, bows nocked, leaving Hunter alone on the floor. He props himself up. His shoulders heave, his breathing worse.

Maybe I will end up killing him.

He climbs stiffly to his feet and trails out of the door, wings drooped. The other angels have scattered, launching into the sky as soon as they reached the forecourt. Hunter leaps awkwardly into flight and disappears in a couple of powerful flaps. I squash a blip of pity.

He's an angel, for goodness' sake. Pitying him will get me killed.

8

The gas and electricity run out within days of each other during my first week at Newhailes. I miss the screens and their comforting glow, plus the fact I could spy on anything going on in the house without leaving the safety of the room.

I've become more reclusive after my clash with Hunter. He left spots of blood that have dried to grey on the carpet.

Did he die?

The security room is black without the screens so I've turned into a bit of a larva, curled in my sleeping bag, reading by the lights of candles and torches. The solar lamps come in handy as I can leave one charging on a window ledge while I use the other so I don't go crazy and start whispering to myself in the dark.

I posted the video of a wounded Hunter to Twitter and every news site, forum or discussion board that was available the night of our sword battle. I messaged it to every contact in my phone, though there weren't many. Old friends whose numbers have probably changed, work colleagues, Steph.

My father.

The message read:

'The fight back starts now.

Use iron and rusted steel.
#angelsofdeath #apocalypse'

I silenced the notifications after they blew up my phone. Images poured in of people fighting with swords, pokers, spears and an honest-to-God cannon. Angels bled. People died. Even with the iron, they struggled to get close enough to deal a fatal blow. But our deaths were no longer easy.

All while I hide under the covers like a child.

I should be out there, fighting alongside my fellow humans, charging the enemy with my sword raised. They've come out of hiding because of me. They're dying because of me, because I gave them hope. I should have at least killed Hunter. If he's still alive, who knows how many people he's dusted.

As if an angel could understand mercy.

I leave the room to use the toilet and wash, the plumbing still working at least. Outside, it's a beautiful winter's day—clear and sunny, frost in the shadows.

"Go, you coward," I whisper to myself.

The insanity begins.

I creep onto the gravel. No arrows sing at me from the trees, only birds. I squeeze the pommel of my sword until my hand cramps. Dew licks my boots, the sun on my face. I breathe gulps of fresh, chilled air.

Nothing has stumbled into my traps, which is just as well since I haven't checked them for days, though I could do with the protein.

I stick to the woods, inhaling the mulchy, damp smell and watching the birds flit between bared branches. The exercise feels good after being cooped up. Almost normal.

Shouts echo from beyond the trees, towards the Forth.

40

Jeering laughter. The rattle of metal. I sneak closer and peek through the waxy-green leaves of a rhododendron. A spider takes the huff and scuttles to the edge of its web, beads of frozen moisture sparkling on the strands.

A figure struggles on the ground in the middle of a field, shackled at wrist and ankle by chains attached to stakes in the dirt. Another stake pins each black wing, driven straight through the flesh and feathers.

Hunter.

Three men prance around him, dressed in camouflage gear, war paint smeared on their cheeks. A man with a dagger pauses every few seconds to mock the pinioned angel and stab. Stab-slash-stab. The man drags the blade in a shallow slice along Hunter's chest, the angel's skin already slick and silver and frothy. No fancy sealing. Shreds of black flutter in the grass from the remains of Hunter's top. He says something in his own language—strangely musical despite the fact it's probably curse words—and bucks against the chains, his heels furrowing the dirt. The people crouch around him. The man with the dagger eases the blade between Hunter's ribs, like I did.

"Rot in hell, angel prick," he says.

Hunter yanks on the shackles, his face pale and desperate. A stake flies loose. His freed hand plucks it in mid-air and rams it into the dagger-man's eye. Hunter slashes the throat of another. The last man spins to flee but Hunter tugs the dagger from his side and throws it. The blade sinks into the man's back and he drops to the ground.

In the silence, Hunter puts his hand over his face and makes a sound between a sigh and a groan. Blood glistens on his chest and belly, running in rivulets down his heaving sides to shimmer on the grass. A dangerous sensation tugs at my stomach.

Stupid pity.

"Looks like you're having a bad day," I say, and step from the shelter of the trees.

Hunter scrabbles for the stake. His shoulder jerks up as far as his pinned wings allow, his body twisted towards me. A fresh wave of blood dampens the waistband of his trousers. His eyes are bright, dry, drowning dark. I sheath my sword. He pants at me, his hair dishevelled and falling over his forehead. There's a smear of silver on his cheek.

It's the most distressed I've ever seen one of them.

A shudder ripples through him. He blinks and puts on his arrogant face.

"It seems," he says very carefully, "they did not know about mercy."

"Can you blame them?"

"We do not torture you."

"We still end up dead. And no one wants to die."

I approach slowly. Dark eyes track me, the stake pointed and unwavering. I pat the pockets of the man with the dagger and find a penknife—useless, uncorroded steel—and a crumpled wad of ten pound notes. I search the others and slide the iron dagger into my boot.

Where is everyone finding these ancient weapons?

"No key," I say, crouched near Hunter's feet. "I'd appreciate it if you wouldn't skewer me through the eyeball with that thing."

I kick at the stake attached to his ankle by a length of chain. The metal hurts the sole of my foot but I keep kicking until it loosens and scrapes from the hard ground. The stake is cold and rough in my hands. Hunter's leg twitches but he doesn't boot me in the face. I do the same for the other ankle and crawl around his wing to the stake spreading his arm wide. Hunter stays very still. Only his eyes move. He keeps his grip on his weapon, practically cuddling it, his knuckles white. The stake attached to his wrist jerks out, though he's still pinned like a butterfly on display.

"These are going to hurt," I say.

I brace a foot on either side of one spread-eagled wing. Rust flakes onto the black of Hunter's feathers. Silver blood has crusted around the edge. I heave but the stake stays fast. Hunter hisses through his teeth.

"Sorry," I say. "I'm going to have to wiggle it."

He fixes his gaze on the sky. "Do it."

I throw my weight against the metal then pull it back. Push, pull, twist. It takes a couple of tries and bruises my shoulders, my palms. Hunter clenches his jaw but says nothing. Finally, the stake slides loose, the tip smeared with mud and frothy blood. I toss it in the grass and repeat the process with the second. A downy, black feather sticks to the edge. Hunter leaps to his feet.

Or I assume this was the aim.

His knees buckle. Chains rattle. I catch him, avoiding the swinging stakes, and slot my shoulder in his armpit. His skin is slick under my hands. Hot.

I've never touched an angel before. He smells of metal and ice.

"Easy," I say. "No sudden moves."

He jerks away and my palms slip in his blood. My skin tingles and I remember my acid theory. I wait for excruciating pain and burning but it stays a mild, not unpleasant prickle.

"I do not need help," Hunter growls, though it's a little slurred. "I do not need—"

Thudding to his hands and knees cuts off the indignant words. He pants at the grass, his head bowed. Narrow leaves stick to the pale skin of his back, his wings held loosely, as if it hurts to fold them.

"Look, we've been out here long enough," I say. "I'm surprised the kerfuffle hasn't attracted attention of the human or angel variety, neither of which I want to deal with."

"We are not..." He shakes his head. "What is kerfuffle?"

I scan the field but it's empty. Nothing moves in the tree line.

"Can you bleed to death?" I say to the genuflecting angel.

"No," he grunts, "but the ground is spinning and I feel... sick."

Iron poisoning? All that cloudy, yellowish froth doesn't look healthy.

"Have you never been hurt like this before?"

He tentatively touches his wounds. "Not like this."

"So quit being stubborn and let me help you."

I hold out my hand. He raises his head to glare. His shoulders bunch and he shoves to his knees. His foot slips in blood and he slumps on his hands, the manacles blanching his wrists. He curses in a way I assume is quite colourful, though I can't understand it.

"You don't want me to touch you—I get it. But you're not walking away from here unless I do. Believe me, if any other human comes along, they're not going to touch you as gently."

Something flickers across Hunter's face. He waves his hand in my general direction without looking at me, the stake swinging from his wrist. I catch his fingers and pull him to his feet. He sways.

"Put your arm across my shoulders. I'm going to put my arm around your back, okay?"

He nods. Silky-soft feathers brush my skin next to the hard

ridge of muscle. Cold metal flops down my side. I steer Hunter into the trees, a stake slapping against my leg with each step. He sags into me but manages to shuffle his feet, chains dragging, his wings drooped and trailing in the leaves.

"You *are* really light. I could pick you up."

He spears me a look from midnight-blue eyes framed by black lashes.

"Do not dare," he says.

He flops more than climbs over the wall, clanking into the forecourt of Newhailes. His skin has turned an ashen grey-green.

"You came back here," he mumbles. "We searched but found no sign."

"You searched after I stabbed you? You could barely breathe."

He shrugs. "The job... was not finished."

"Well, I never left. I gambled on you assuming I'd run."

Something rumbles in his chest, not strong enough to reach his mouth.

"Clever," he says.

I hoist his limp body up the steps to the main entrance, the servants' door wedged by the bookcase again. The stakes attached to his ankles ring on the stone. I kick the door shut behind us and aim him across the lobby. His hand flaps on my shoulder.

"What are they doing?"

I glance at the painting above the fireplace. "Kissing. Angels don't kiss?"

"We are not angels."

"So what are you?"

"The Protectorate."

I shove him sideways up the slightly spiralling steps to the second floor. "No, I mean, if we're human, what are you?"

"The Protectorate," he says.

I sigh. "Fine. The Protectorate don't kiss?"

Shadows hood his face in the dim corridor. His eyes flash in the darkness.

"No," he says.

Funny, I swear he's looking at my mouth.

9

There's an angel sprawled on the floor of my security room. He takes up a lot of space.

I light my candles in a ring around Hunter until it looks like I'm about to perform a sacrifice. Shadows pool in his cheekbones. He's darkness covered in blood and metal.

I pack towels and sheets around him and fill every container I can find with water. He shivers when I sluice off the blood. If it's iron toxicity making him sick and woozy, I'm hoping that washing the froth and cloudy fluid away will treat it. What else can I do in this apocalypse his kind created? I pat him dry and dress his wounds, sealing the deeper cuts with butterfly stitches then micropore tape when those run out. My hands tingle. He watches me through half-lidded eyes and finally stops shuddering under my fingers.

"Why do you help me?" he says.

I pause in my ministrations.

It's a damn good question. He'd just been so distressed lying in the field in shackles. Hurt and alone. Helping him seemed like the right thing to do.

Steph would have a few stern words about my behaviour, no doubt.

"Maybe it's time we find a better solution than killing each other," I say.

"Was it you who spread the message to the rest?" Hunter says. "The video of me?"

I focus on my hands smoothing bandages on his ribs. "It was me."

"You made everything worse."

I frown at him. "Well, sorry, but I think you had it pretty sodding easy up to that point."

His head lolls. He may be expressing disagreement but I can't quite tell.

"Worse for the Protectorate also," he sighs, his eyes closed, "but I was talking about me."

"What do you mean?"

His chest rises and falls beneath my hands.

"Hunter?"

No answer. Probably best not to poke him.

I finish covering his wounds and seal the rents in his wings. Sitting back on my heels, I take a minute just to look at him.

Sleep softens the arrogance from his face. Solid muscle broadens his chest and shoulders, presumably to help with flight. Narrow hips and long, slim legs. His black trousers lace up the sides all the way from his black, knee-high boots to his waist. Even the crotch is laced.

Stop looking at his crotch.

I bet he has nothing there. What does a species created for war need a penis for, anyway? Surely, it would only be a distraction.

I find myself petting his feathers.

Stop that, too.

I watch him breathe for a while. He breathes like a human. I press my ear to the woven bandages on his chest. He has a heart and it beats like a human's.

The wings flopped flat and spanning the room, not so much.

What the hell am I doing with a wounded angel? I really didn't think this through. Didn't think at all, in fact.

I leave him to his slumber and risk a breathless ten-minute jog along Newhailes Road to a hardware shop further west towards Edinburgh. The boltcutters cleave Hunter's manacles better than the rusty saw I found in a drawer. It scraped the metal, the vibration buzzing in my teeth, then snapped.

I toss the stakes and chains in a corner. Raw, weeping skin bands Hunter's wrists and I bandage them, too. At least his boots protected his ankles.

I make food, potter around, read and get ready for bed in my nook under the control desk. I wheel the chair in front of me as if it will be any kind of barrier should Hunter wake in a human-killing mood.

My sword stays close. Hunter doesn't stir.

Maybe he'll die this time. I'll open my eyes in the morning and find him cold and stiff.

* * *

But he's not, though he is still unconscious. He remains comatose for two days and is immune to external stimuli.

Okay, so I poke him a little.

He may have slept longer but I accidentally step on his wing and he startles awake.

Why the wing and not the poke? A mystery.

His eyes appear black in the gloom of one solar light. He tracks me without moving any other part of his body as I sit in the chair and tuck my knees to my chest, blowing on my tea.

He reminds me of some exotic cat. One that's trying to decide whether to eat me or not.

Though the wings don't fit the analogy.

My heart rate climbs while he stays silent and watches me. He sits in a rustle of feathers and bandages. I flinch but manage not to spill my tea. He glances down at his freed wrists and ankles, the patchwork I've made of his torso. He picks at the edge of a dressing.

"Don't touch," I say a little too harshly. "You need to let it heal."

He gives me his arrogant face, all lines and darkness.

"What?" I say. "You don't like being told what to do?"

"I am created to follow orders," he says, one black brow raised, "just not from humans."

"Yeah, well, get used to it. You're the only angel here."

"I am not—"

"Fine," I sigh, "you're not an angel. You look like one, though, and Protectorate is too much of a mouthful."

He frowns at me. I give him a placid smile and sip my tea. Sweet and black.

Not like a certain angel I could mention.

"Do you want some tea? Breakfast?"

"I do not need to eat."

"You don't eat?"

"I do not *need* to eat. The mission bolus lasts a few months." He narrows his eyes at me. "We thought we would be finished with time to spare."

"Don't blame me. If you really were created, they gave you a weakness to iron or iron oxide. Maybe they wanted something to control you if you got dangerous."

"We *are* dangerous."

He fixes me with his panther eyes, his wings slightly spread, the bandages bright in the centre of each. One leg is straight, the other bent, his trousers low on his hips.

I slurp another mouthful of hot liquid. "So where are we on the tea?"

He cocks his head. The silence wriggles into my belly.

I wish he wouldn't stare at me. It's like he can see my insides.

"I will have tea," he finally says.

I stand up and step towards the door, angling around him. He leaps to his feet.

Considering he's been comatose and recumbent for the last two days, I'm surprised he does nothing but wobble a bit.

I move to help and he lurches away, his back thudding into the door. He hisses and holds a hand to his side.

"If you'd quit jerking around, you wouldn't hurt yourself."

"I am not jerking around."

"You also need to work on your conversation skills and not just disagree with everything I say."

"I do not—"

He shuts his mouth and scowls at me. I manage to swallow a laugh.

"You're quite prickly, aren't you?" I say.

"What is prickly?"

"You'll figure it out."

I shoo him away from the door. He slides to the side and kicks the solar light, plunging the room into blackness. My heart leaps into my mouth.

I'm trapped with an angel, and blind.

Can he see me? Is he moving?

I take a few deep breaths.

"Okay, stay still." My voice is about two decibels higher. "And don't break me into pieces if I touch you accidentally."

I place my cup on the ground and crawl to where I think the lamp rolled. Hunter is invisible but I feel him, the heat and weight of him, looming over me. His eyes are on me. My pulse flutters on my tongue.

This is ridiculous. But I really want the light on.

My hand brushes something firm yet pliant. Criss-crossing material.

"Is this your foot?"

"Yes," he says, his soft voice in the darkness sending a little shiver through me.

He doesn't smell like metal anymore. Just ice. Crisp and clean. Like sucking on an icicle, the cold sliding deep into your belly.

So how is he warm? He's a slightly bigger, way more intense replacement to the electric heater that no longer works.

My fingers nudge a round object. I snatch it and light floods the room.

I'm kneeling at Hunter's feet. It takes a while for my gaze to travel up his long body and meet his eyes, watching me. Sharp eyes, sharp cheekbones.

"Can you see in the dark?"

He smirks. "Yes."

"Bastard," I mutter.

I lead him to the conservatory, detouring through the kitchen to make him tea and refresh mine. He takes it black, sniffing the steam. We sit on either end of a couch facing the windows and the lawn. A pigeon pecks at something in the grass.

"I am surprised you have not been spotted," he says, sipping, then wrinkling his nose.

"The glass is tinted. You can't see inside unless you press

your face to it. Do you want some sugar?"

"What is sugar?"

"It sweetens the tea."

He holds out his cup. I accept it, careful not to brush his fingers and inspire another leap towards the ceiling. In the kitchen, I add a teaspoon of sugar and return to the couch. He cradles the cup, his wings arching over the sofa back. The bandages make his feathers darker.

"Will anyone come looking for you?"

His eyes meet mine, perfectly blank.

"No," he says.

"Where were you created?"

"Far away."

"In a galaxy far, far away?"

He cocks his head. "Yes."

"I was quoting—never mind. This galaxy where you were created—it's in a whole other universe separate to this one?"

"There are many universes separate to this one."

"Like multiple dimensions? Are they copies of this universe? Are there copies of me?"

Hunter takes another experimental sip of tea and his eyes widen. He peers into his cup then drains half of it, licking his lips.

"Not copies," he finally says. "Infinite versions—some like here, some very different."

"How can you travel between them? We didn't even know they were there. I mean, scientists hypothesised about the multiverse with cosmic inflation and quantum nature, string theory..."

I trail off, the physics of multiple universes lost on me.

"We use portals."

"Portals?" I wiggle my fingers. "Let me guess—ripples in the fabric of space-time."

Hunter cocks his head again. "Yes."

Jeez, I was joking.

I shift on the couch and tuck my legs underneath me so I can face him without twisting. He tenses until I settle.

"What's the name of your planet?"

"I do not have a planet."

"Then where do you live?"

"On a ship."

My word, it's like pulling the stakes all over again. Maybe he's punishing me for mocking his conversation skills.

We finish our tea and walk through the lobby, past the painting—the kiss—he was so fascinated with. I catch him glancing at it. Back in the security room, he stretches out on the floor and stares at the ceiling. I switch on a solar torch and lock the door. The soft light suits him. Blackness and shadows.

Was the room always this small?

I clear my throat. "I could get you some blankets to lie on. Maybe a mattress."

"I am used to lying on the ground."

"Okay, but you don't have to. You can be comfortable."

"I am comfortable."

I'm not. It was less disconcerting when he was unconscious.

I flop into the chair and wince at the creak, loud in the cramped space. "So, what do you do when you're not depopulating broken planets?"

He tilts his head to look at me. "Train for the next battle."

"Don't you do anything for fun?"

"We train. We compete. We service our creators. We couple."

"Couple?"

He gives me blank, dark eyes. Heat blooms in my cheeks.

"Couple—gotcha. No need for details."

I guess he does have a penis.

I grab a book to give my hands something to do.

"You can read?" he says after a while.

"You can't?"

"No."

Then how does he know so much about us? His English is perfect. He's familiar with our culture and technology. If he was created, was all this knowledge fed directly into his brain?

Humans are not that different. My ex-boyfriends certainly preferred sex to a good book.

So I read to the angel lying on the floor.

10

Hunter stares at me like I'm a sparrowhawk and he's the pigeon about to be devoured. He's sitting in the wheeled chair, his wings flopped in the gaps between the seat back and the arm rests.

He fell asleep while I was reading to him yesterday. His breathing deepened. His eyelids fluttered, then slipped shut. His muscles relaxed, one by one. I wanted to yawn just watching him.

The book was a paranormal romance about fairies. Raunchy fairies, though thankfully it was a tame bit. Violence and court intrigue instead of hot sex. The hot sex comes later.

Oh, crap. What if he wants me to read more?

"I'm going to change your bandages," I say. "It shouldn't hurt."

I kneel between his legs. His wings flare out. The tips of his feathers brush through a candle flame. He hisses and jerks his wings back.

"You felt that?"

"We feel pain," he says stiffly, drawing his wings in tight.

"So all the weapons the army fired at you guys…"

"Hurt."

"Huh," I say, and peel a bandage off, being as gentle as

possible.

His fingers tense on the arm rests. Plastic creaks in protest.

I forget about his hatred of proximity when I uncover the wound. I lean closer to peer at it in the dim light. Hunter goes completely rigid, as if he wants to launch out of the chair but my head is in the way. His crotch would smack me in the face.

"This looks over a week old," I gasp, and realise I'm breathing on him. "You've healed fast."

"This is slow," he says through his teeth.

I blink at him. "Normal injures heal faster than this?"

"In hours, not days. Only bone takes longer."

"Have you broken many bones?"

"Yes," he says.

I lift my t-shirt. "This is where you cut me after a week."

A scabbed line traces my ribs where he grazed me with his knife in the servants' corridor. I glance at him and miss something in his face before it shifts to a painfully arrogant expression. His cheekbones are sharp enough to pierce his skin, his eyes slitted.

"Would you relax?" I say. "I'm not doing anything bad."

I drop my shirt and pick another bandage off while he vibrates with tension.

"It must take a lot of energy to heal so fast," I say, keeping my voice pleasant and low. "Is that why you were unconscious for two days?"

"Yes. Healing. Leaves us vulnerable."

"And yet I managed not to molest you. I guess you can trust me."

Except for the poking, but he doesn't need to know about that.

His eyes search my face. "Trust you?"

"Yes, Hunter—generally when you nurse a man back to health, you expect a degree of trust."

"I am not a man."

I roll my eyes. "Like the angel thing—without the wings and, okay, the super-healing and semi-invincibility—you're close enough."

I remove the rest of the dressings. Hunter manages not to catapult himself out of the chair.

"You don't even have a scar where I stabbed you and I bet all these will fade, too."

Whoops. My hands are splayed on his ribs.

Man, he's solid.

I raise my head and meet his eyes and, for a second, there's something there, something *hungry*.

I stop touching him.

He spreads each wing and I pluck the bandages off, trying not to take a clump of feathers with them. I smooth the ruffles in the softness over delicate bones and skin.

"I haven't seen anyone else with this colour. Most of you are gold and white."

"I am the only one."

"Does that mean you're special?"

"No," he says.

Wow. Talking to him is like our sword battle, except it's me trying to batter him into submission.

"Do you want to go for a walk? Not outside. The house is big enough, you can get a decent stroll going."

"I need clothes," he says.

"Oh, right, sorry. I think I have something..."

I rifle through my various provisions and scoop up the shirt I took from the abandoned holdall in Musselburgh.

"Look," I say, waving it at him, "it's in your colour."

He treats me to a Hunter stare.

"What?" I say. "You can't deny you've got a dark, smouldering thing going on."

He snatches the shirt from my grip and slides his arms through the sleeves. The material bunches over his wings, the tails caressing his ribs.

"Hmm, needs some adjustment but I don't think I have scissors…" I pick up my sword. "Hold still."

He lunges backwards. "No."

"I'm not going to cut you. Just quit jerking about."

"I am *not*—"

His teeth click shut. He balls his hands into fists and turns around. I tug the material as far down as I can get it. It whispers over his wings.

"Don't move," I say.

I make two slits in the back of the shirt from the hem towards the neck and tuck them in so Hunter's wings pop through. The material is a little squint on one side.

"Can you crouch down?"

He tosses me a scowl over his shoulder.

"You're too tall. I'm almost done."

He squats. I ease the blade higher so both slits are even.

"There. Do you want me to pin it so it doesn't flap?"

"No," he says.

He fastens the buttons, the silky material tight across his shoulders and biceps, and leaves it untucked. The hollow of his throat shows at the collar. Back to warrior in black. Now all he needs is a bow and arrows.

Or maybe not.

We tour the first and second floors, the air damp and chilly.

Hunter glances at the empty glass case in the library then at the sword on my belt. The second sword sits in its box where I left it. He trails his fingers along the rows of ancient books. The sun sets in the tree line, slanting orange beams through the mullioned windows.

"If you guys can see in the dark, why do you never hunt at night?" I say.

He wipes his dusty fingers on his trousers, leaving grey streaks. "Night is for checking scores. And celebrating the tally."

"How fun."

"It is not fun."

"And does the angel with the highest score get a prize?"

I push out into the passageway and we wind our way down through the kitchen to the maze of servants' corridors. I turn on my torch to banish the dark.

"They get what they want," Hunter says, as if I asked the question a second ago.

I turn and the beam of light flashes across his face. He doesn't even squint, his pupils pinpoints, the midnight-blue bright under the light. I expect to see stars sparkling in there.

"And what is that?" I say.

"Whatever they want."

So more sex then.

War and sex. What a way to live.

My torch plays over the drab walls and brown carpet. I turn a corner and something swirls in the shadows—an arrow. Embedded in the wall at a sharp angle. Shot at me while I dived around the corner.

Sweat pops out on my forehead. I retreat and Hunter sidesteps to avoid me crashing into his chest. His wings rustle on the wallpaper.

I forgot about the arrows. The first he fired in the lobby had disappeared so I assumed the rest were collected.

Hunter plucks the arrow and rolls it between his fingers. The tip glows blue and the colour swirls along the shaft. His eyes meet mine, dark and alien.

Has this all been a trap? He's healed but he hasn't said anything about returning to his people or more on why I rescued him and what we should do about it. Are we saving the world or just ourselves?

To be honest, I'm a bit out of my depth. I have no plan. I just felt sorry for him.

Sorry for an angel. What an idiot.

Hunter twirls the arrow against his finger and the tip dents his skin. My stomach rolls. The blue swirls, fast and faster. I brace a hand on the wall.

"Do you know," he says, his voice soft and bland, "there are some tasked with culling the creatures you call cattle and sheep?"

I slide back a step. Another. My spine hits the wall.

Too far.

"No, I didn't know that." My voice, unlike Hunter's, could shatter glass.

My torch beam wobbles on his feet, slanting shadows in his cheekbones. Black hair falls into black eyes. His wings fill the width of the corridor and almost touch the ceiling. I try to merge with the wallpaper.

Hunter claims a step. "They are having an easier time."

My stomach clenches and shoots bile into my throat.

"I saw that redhead hit you," I say in a rush. "In the lobby."

He stops moving towards me. The arrow spins through his

slim fingers. He cocks his head, like a raven before it pecks out my eye.

Do ravens do that?

"Doesn't she like you?"

"No," he says.

"Why not?"

His gaze drops to my hand on the pommel of my sword, my knuckles white.

He's too close for me to draw it in time. I've wedged myself into the opposite corner from where the arrow has left a divot in the wall.

"I do not fit in," he says, and snaps the shaft in two.

My breath whooshes out, taking the strength from my legs with it. I sag against the wall.

Hunter smirks. "It is called trust, Maia."

He drops the arrow, both halves a dull black. No more evil, soul-sucking, swirly blue.

"Yeah, well," I pant, "maybe you shouldn't be all intense and ominous and I wouldn't get confused."

I quit shivering against the wall like an injured mouse. I sidle around Hunter and the broken arrow and continue down the corridor.

"What do you call those things?"

"Soulreavers."

"Have you used them in other universes?"

"We use them everywhere."

"Are other civilisations really that similar?"

"Every living creature has a soul." His eyes meet mine, black in the dimness. "Except me."

I swallow and my throat clicks. "How old are you, Hunter?"

Is he as ancient as the sword in my hand? More?

"I am the newest," he says.

I sheath my blade. "What does that mean?"

"Our creators experimented with a different strain."

"So you and all the angels with wings other than white or gold...?"

"Are the latest creations."

I weave through the corridors towards the stairs to the lobby. Hunter is silent behind me except for the occasional whisper of his feathers.

"And how does that work—one day you just open your eyes and *poof,* you're aware?"

"Yes," he says.

What a harsh start to life. From his first breath, he became a weapon. A warrior. Nothing as simple as a childhood to have fun before the adult worries wore you down. Only battle and death.

My eyes scan the walls and stairs for another glimpse of swirly blue.

"Would I get sucked into a soulreaver if I only touched the shaft?"

"No, the tip needs to taste skin."

I shudder. "Those things are never tasting my skin."

He gives me a considering look and I spend the walk to the security room trying to puzzle it out.

Like I could possibly understand what goes on in his head.

11

"This ship you live on, what's it like?"

I'm lying in the centre of the room on the pillow and air mattress I've dragged out from my nook under the control desk. Hunter sits in the chair, swivelling back and forth with his toes on the floor.

He still hasn't taken off his boots. He sleeps in them.

Maybe angels don't unwind. Or he has foot fungus.

"Big," he says.

"Come on, Hunter—I know you can say more than one-word sentences."

"It is extremely big," he says with no change in tone or expression.

"Hilarious. Do you not have a planet you can go to? You know, for some rest and relaxation?"

"I am on a planet now."

"Oh, yes, very relaxing."

I prop myself on my elbows. He keeps swinging the chair but his eyes stay on me.

"Sometimes," he says, stretching the word out, "we are invited to the planets of our creators."

"Planets? You mean more than one civilisation contributed? Is this in one universe or many?"

"My universe is the first. Many planets are inhabited."

"How do you know you're the first?"

He levels me a stare. "We are the first."

"Do any of the civilisations look like you?"

"No."

I watch him and wave my hand in an encouraging motion.

He sighs. "Some are winged but less humanoid, like our creators."

"See, we're making progress. Why did they make you look like angels?"

He frowns at his boots. "This image is accepted in many universes and does not provoke an immediate response."

"How many universes have you been to?"

His gaze meets mine. "I do not count."

"You seem to count everything else," I mutter then flap my hand at his cocked head. "What about the universes that don't believe in angels or heaven or whatever?"

"Other creations are deployed. My form is only one faction."

I jerk upright. "There are more creations that don't look like you?"

"Our creators build whatever is required. We are the oldest. Our form is... favoured."

A shiver runs down my spine. "So, getting invited to their planets, is that part of servicing your creators? What does that even mean—you wash their clothes?"

Hunter snorts.

"Cut their grass?" I continue. "Polish their car? Or are they robots that need an oil change every few months?"

His heels hit the carpet. He sits forward, elbows on his knees. His wings cast massive shadows on the wall.

"Are these terms for coupling?"

I gape at him then remind myself to shut my mouth.

"Do you guys hump everything when you're not waging war on wayward societies?"

He slumps in the chair. His gaze rises to the patterns of light and dark on the ceiling, which is a break from him trying to bore through my brain with his eyeballs.

"It is an honour to be selected."

"Said in a tone by someone who disagrees."

He rolls his head on the seat and pins me with his eyes. "There was no change in tone."

"They built you so they're entitled to sample the merchandise? That's creepy."

"They are our creators. They can do what they want."

"You guys are semi-invincible warrior angels. What about what you want?"

"A weapon does not want."

He doesn't look like a weapon. Sprawled in the chair, long, slim legs spread, his stare unflinching from behind the hair flopped over his forehead. He steeples his hands on his flat stomach and watches me watch him. Predatory. Intense. But not a weapon.

Or not just a weapon.

"Were you selected?" I say quietly.

If I hadn't been studying his face for the last few days, and the infinitesimal movements he calls expressions, I probably would've missed the tiny flinch. Instead of yelling, "Ah-*ha!*" and brandishing a finger, I move onto my side and prop my head on my fist. I breathe and wait.

"It is an honour," he says stiffly, his eyes narrowed.

"You're the only angel here. You don't have to parrot the party line."

"I do not understand what you mean."

"Your English is advanced, Hunter. You know what I mean."

He gives me an arrogant stare in lieu of rebuttal.

I roll my eyes. "You said it yourself—you don't fit in. Would any other angel sit and talk to me like this?"

I take his silence as a no.

"And maybe you're the misfit who also thinks you shouldn't be whored out to your creators."

He scowls. "Non-conformity is nothing to be proud of."

"Why not? If they wanted you to conform, they would've made you pretty and dumb. You're obviously not dumb. Unless you're the black sheep for that, too."

He blinks at me and seems to wrestle with a few responses in his head. I enjoy watching them shuttle across his face. The more annoyed he gets, the less he hides, though he may end up punching me and putting me in a coma.

It's a risk.

"Are all humans like you?" he says.

"Like what?"

He mulls this over. I wish I knew what he was thinking, though I imagine most of it would terrify me.

He settles on, "Irritating."

"It's called curiosity, Hunter," I say, and smirk at him.

He wriggles higher in the chair and slides his arms onto the rests, drumming his fingers on the ends. He has beautiful hands, for a warrior.

"You said they would have made me pretty and dumb but I am not dumb." He skewers me with his gaze again. "So, I am pretty?"

Oh, balls. Caught in my own word play.

"Well, you're not ugly…"

"I am built for war, why would they make me pretty?"

"Because they don't want to bang some hulking troll?"

His mouth works but no sound comes out. He alternates between screwing up his face, like he's about to say something profound, and blinking. He cocks his head, as if that will help. I put my hand over my mouth to hide my grin but a snort slips out.

A full-on bemused Hunter. It's kind of cute.

"What is bang?" he says.

I laugh for a very long time. And I've not laughed for what seems like a *very* long time.

I come to flopped on the mattress, giggling at the ceiling. My stomach hurts. I whoop in a gulp of air and it sniggers out. Tears blur my eyes.

"Oh man, I needed that," I hiccup. "You're so bloody serious. Everything's so bloody serious and depressing."

"Are you dying?"

Hunter kneels on the floor, half-way between the chair and where I'm currently wobbling like a jellyfish. His wings arch towards me, shimmering with purple and green in the light.

Why have I never noticed that before?

I raise my hand and brush my fingertips through silky feathers. Hunter freezes.

I snatch my hand back. "Sorry. Wasn't thinking."

"Why do you always touch?"

It's more curious than admonitory.

He settles his wings carefully against his back. I turn my head to keep him in view as he reverses into the chair, his eyes on me.

"Humans are a tactile species. Don't angels do causal touching when they're not shagging each other?"

"Shagging?"

"Sex. Coupling sounds too mechanical."

"We touch only for competition and... sex." He rolls the word in his mouth like it's a sweet he's never tasted before.

The way he says it gives me goosebumps. With his soft voice and dark, intense eyes, he would be great at dirty talk.

"No hand-holding?" I say, shoving the sleeves of my over-sized hoodie to my elbows.

It suddenly got warm in here, and that's saying something with Hunter the walking space-heater.

"Why would we hold hands? Unless to pin or grapple an opponent."

"Hugging?"

"What is hugging?"

I thrust myself to a sitting position and cross my legs.

"You've never had a hug?"

"I do not know what it is."

"When someone puts their arms around you and holds you close." I mimic it in the air.

"To get you to submit?"

"No, to comfort. To be intimate. You hug someone when you like them. Don't you hug after sex?"

"No," he says.

"Jeez. So just wham, bam, thank you, ma'am? Sounds cold."

"Humans do not do this?"

"Well, sometimes. But usually there's hand-holding, hugging, kissing, touching. Displays of affection."

He scans me from top to toe but not like a warrior assessing for weaknesses. This focuses on the softer bits—breasts, hips.

Crap, I'm sitting cross-legged.

I fold my knees to my chest. I'm not exactly a glowing

example of womanhood with my hair pinned on top of my head, strands curling to my shoulders, and a baggy hoodie, plus jeans that are a little dirty and my red socks with a hole in the toe.

When did I last bathe?

And why am I discussing tenderness and intimacy with an angel? Clearly, it's not in his DNA, if he even has DNA.

I lick my lips. "What are you thinking?"

Hunter raises his implacable gaze to my face and, as usual, says nothing.

12

I decide to read after ten minutes of Hunter watching me in silence, like I'm an alien creature he's struggling to understand. Though I guess I am.

Well, he can dissect my brain with his eyeballs while I'm reading. At least my attention will be elsewhere.

I regret my decision after the first couple of pages. Damn raunchy fairies. I should skip over it. Like Hunter's going to know I missed a chunk.

No. I'm an adult. I'm not embarrassed. Plus, he was the one fascinated by the painting of a kiss.

This'll give him something to ponder.

I bend my head over the book to avoid Hunter's gaze, though the weight of it caresses my skin. My cheeks flush and I'm grateful for the dimness until I remember he can see in the dark. I may as well be under a spotlight. I frown at the words on the page to avoid looking at him.

The main character is in the surf. Her fairy lover picks her up easily, his hands cradling her back, her knees on his shoulders. He licks between her legs.

"He is weaker then?" Hunter says.

I jump at his soft voice gliding out of the shadows. My fingers clench on the pages and the book tumbles into my lap.

71

It takes me two tries to say, "Weaker?" and it wobbles along with my heartbeat.

Hunter is sprawled in the chair, a picture of relaxation, but there's a tension in him, vibrating beneath the surface.

"The weaker uses their mouth. The dominant always receives."

Oh, jeez—I'm talking oral sex with an angel.

I clear my throat. "It's more of a give and take."

"The dominant only take."

His dark eyes pin me. All the air seems to have been sucked from the room. He watches me with a predator's hunger and I'm very aware of all my throbbing places.

"Do you like to dominate, Hunter?" The words slip out, husky in the small, intimate space.

His wings flare. The tips brush a pile of cans near the wall and they clatter to the floor, several rolling to bump against the wheels of the chair. It breaks my gaze from his and I can breathe again. I focus on gathering the tins into a pyramid, grabbing the ones around Hunter's seat without looking at him.

He's definitely looking at me.

"Let's play cards," I say, and snatch the cardboard packet.

"What is cards?"

"A game."

"Does it test strength or stamina?"

"Neither."

"Then what is its purpose?"

I roll my eyes. "Fun. It's about time you experienced it."

A pressure in my chest eases and my heart settles to where it belongs instead of pulsing in places it shouldn't.

I'm curious but not *that* curious.

I shuffle the cards and deal two opposite piles. "You need to come sit down here."

Hunter cocks his head. After his usual ten million minutes of silent regard that does nothing for my blood pressure, he slides from the chair and squats on his haunches more than an arm's length away.

"Would you sit like a normal person?" I sigh. "Here."

I toss my pillow and he catches it.

"I am not a person."

"No shit but you have an arse so park it."

He places the pillow a little closer and perches on it. I explain the rules of *Snap*. He raises his gaze from the cards to my face.

"What do I get if I win?"

"What do you usually get?"

More silence. More staring. His eyes are black, more pupil than iris.

"Whatever I want," he says softly.

"Um..." I say. I say it again before I untangle my tongue. "If you win, you get to choose the next game. The next *board* game."

Some games are dangerous.

I flip my first card and nod at Hunter to do the same. Slim fingers flick an ace of clubs into the centre. We pick up a rhythm, the cards whispering against each other. Hunter leans closer, his intensity on the growing pile instead of me for once. It leaves me lightheaded. His hair flops across his forehead. His wings stroke the air and bring his crisp, clean scent.

"Snap!" He slams his hand on the pile.

I jump and swallow a yelp. My pulse bounds into my throat and flops around.

"Well done," I croak. "One point I should mention—try not

to break my hand if we go for the cards at the same time."

He smirks. "Then do not go for the cards."

"Don't get cocky just because you're winning. And if you smash any of my bones, you definitely lose."

He gathers his cards into his pile and the game continues. I win some. He wins some. Okay, he wins most. He has the steely concentration of a warrior angel from a society based on strength and dominance. I have no hope.

Maybe I'll win at *Monopoly* or *Hungry Hippos*.

I hunch over the cards, my muscles rigid. The heat from Hunter bakes me since we're practically nose to nose. Funny he hasn't noticed. At my turn, I yank off my hoodie, scattering the last of the pins in my hair so it tumbles down my back. Cool air teases my bare shoulders and arms, my vest black. Hunter's colour. I flip my card.

"Snap!"

I expect my hand to hit nothing. The last three times, Hunter has swiped the cards before the word even formed on my lips. My palm touches the slick pile. Hunter grabs a second too late. His fingers curl around my hand. His skin is hot, smooth, pliant. No calluses for a species with rapid healing. My head whips up. Hunter stares at me. Close enough to feel him breathing, both of us bent over the cards in the middle.

"Who wins?" he says, his voice quiet and low.

His hand stays on mine. Tingles zip from the press of his skin to the pit of my stomach.

"I do," I whisper and wonder why I'm whispering. "My hand is on the cards."

He glances down, as if he can't tell by the brand of his palm on the back of my hand.

"Did I break anything?"

I wiggle my fingers, trapped by the weight of him. My head shakes my answer, my tongue stuck to the roof of my mouth.

"Good," he says, and lifts his hand.

He wins at *Snap* while I'm still trying to gather myself. We play chess and *Scrabble* and *Hungry Hippos* (my choice). He grins when he beats me. I blink at him. His eyes seem lighter, bluer. A midnight sky graced by the moon. His wings arch when he's hunched over the board, anticipating and eager. They flare and flap when he wins, tease the air when he's deep in thought. They don't droop when he's defeated.

Not here.

"You'd think you'd never won anything before," I grumble when he trounces me at *Connect Four* and sends me reeling with another grin.

The humour leaks to his arrogant face.

"I have not," he says.

A strange pain pinches my heart.

"You must have won battles."

A shrug. "Group effort."

"But you come from a species that thrives on dominance."

He gives me nothing.

"You're scary intimidating," I venture.

Not even a smirk.

"You've never won a competition against another angel?"

Silence.

"You're never dominant, not even at…"

I don't say it out loud. If it's true, what does it mean?

Hunter is a statue of marble skin and shadow. The game sits abandoned in bright rows of yellow and red.

"It means you never get what you want," I breathe.

Finally, he frowns. "How do you know when I say nothing?"

"Women's intuition."

"What is that?"

"A kind of instinct."

He climbs to his feet to tower over me. "I do not like it."

"Sorry. I didn't mean to make you uncomfortable."

I stand slowly to mirror him. He glares at me, his hands at his sides.

He never crosses his arms, not even when he's in a huff. Is it a warrior thing?

"I am not uncomfortable," he says.

Back to clipped sentences. It hurts my chest a little. He was relaxing, having fun, and I ruined it by being a sore loser.

"Can I make it up to you?" I say.

"What does that mean?"

"I want to make you feel better."

"Why?" He cocks his head and my stomach clenches at his appraising look. "How?"

"I'm going to give you a hug."

Appraising slips back to arrogant.

"I do not want a hug."

"How do you know if you've never had one?"

What am I doing? I don't want to cuddle an angel. One squeeze and he'll snap me in two.

I step around *Connect Four*. Or try to. My foot catches the plastic frame and scatters the pieces across the floor.

Now, Hunter smirks at me.

It disappears when I claim another step and we're toe to toe. I have to tilt my head to meet his eyes. His black, wary eyes.

"This won't hurt," I say somewhat hopefully.

It's not him I'm worried about.

He returns to his haughty silence.

"I'd appreciate it if you wouldn't crush me." The words quiver but I ignore it.

I move forward another inch. His hands twitch, held away from his sides. Probably so he can defend himself against the foolish human invading his personal space. I suck in a breath and slide my arms around him. Tension sings in his body. I rest my head on his collarbone and count his heartbeats.

Faster than when he was unconscious.

The warmth of him mixes with his strangely pleasant smell of ice. My hands rest on the thick muscle of his lower back above the silky material of his shirt. They glide upwards and cup the base of his wings where they sprout from his shoulder blades. Downy fluff tickles my skin.

Hunter is so stiff, he's vibrating.

"Tell me you hate it and I'll stop," I mumble into his chest.

His ribs expand and contract under my arms. Also faster than usual. But he stays quiet and he doesn't separate my head from my torso. I take it as a win.

"Or, if you're feeling adventurous, you can put your arms around me. Then it'll be a hug. Right now, it's kind of one-sided." I squeak out a laugh.

Nervous? What do I have to be nervous about? I'm only offering myself to a predator and praying he won't eat me.

Is he moving? I brace for pain. My heart flaps against my sternum, which Hunter can probably feel on his stomach. His very flat, very hard stomach. I've never hugged a man with washboard abs before.

Though he's not a man.

A band of heat hovers over my spine. A gentle palm cups one shoulder blade, his fingers scalding bare skin. The other hand shifts to my lower back. Every muscle in Hunter's body seems to melt. His wings curl around me, as warm and supple as an electric blanket. He rests his cheek on the top of my head and sighs into my hair.

It's the best hug I've ever had. Also, the longest but I dare not move and spoil the moment.

His heart slows and mine matches it. I rub his back and accidentally slip my fingers through the slit in his shirt to stroke skin. His heart speeds. A weird feeling rolls through my stomach and I decide not to examine it too closely. His hand tightens, pressing me against him, no space between the line of his body and mine.

That's probably long enough for a friendly cuddle.

"Hunter?" I whisper.

An enquiring noise rumbles under my ear but, otherwise, he doesn't move.

"Do you think you could pick me up and—"

Suddenly, I'm hoisted aloft and eye to eye with a freaking warrior angel. My hips are tucked against his hips. There's a hand on my arse.

"Not *now!*" I yelp.

He blinks at me. I wriggle in his arms and he lets me go. My feet hit the floor but my legs wobble. I flop onto the air mattress, a hand on my chest like a swooning damsel in a black-and-white movie.

"Jesus," I gasp, too flustered to wince at the blasphemy. "I meant could you pick me up and still be able to fly?"

He looks down at me, all dark eyes and sharp cheekbones. His face is impassive but there's something different. Something that sends nerves and excitement fizzing through my belly.

"Yes," he says. "I can pick you up and fly."

The purr in his voice hints I've stumbled into unknown territory. Dangerously unknown territory.

Oh, Jesus.

What have I started?

13

"This hasn't been some elaborate ruse so you can drop me out of the sky, right?"

Frost crunches under my boots and sparkles silver in the moonlight. I hug myself against the chill, bundled into a couple of sweaters and a jacket. My sword slaps my thigh, safely sheathed.

Hunter arches a brow. "If I wanted to kill you, I would have done it while you slept."

"Somehow, that's comforting," I say.

He snorts and scans the sky, the trees.

What does it look like when you can see in the dark?

He may have been created for war but the night suits him. The moon complements his pale skin, black hair and clothes. Shadows pool beneath the sharp lines of his face and in the hollow of his throat. Moonlight kisses his feathers and shines in his eyes.

"Are you ready?" he says, his gaze back on me.

I should change my mind. Say no. Maybe flying with an angel has some deep significance. Like it's how they choose a mate. Or indicate they want to have sex.

But I'll never get another opportunity like this.

I nod my head, my breath fogging out. Hunter slips behind

me and it's my turn to tense, as stiff as he was yesterday when I, stupidly, thought cuddling an angel was a good idea.

Though he seemed to like it.

His arms wrap around me. He leaps upwards and his wings snap out. I fail to stifle a yelp as the ground drops from my feet and vertigo tugs at my stomach. My fingers dig into his arms.

"Open your eyes, Maia," he says, his lips brushing my ear.

His wings beat against the sky. The whole world smells like him—ice and frost. The air nips at my nose and cheeks and fingers, the rest of me warm wherever Hunter touches.

The still water of the Firth of Forth reflects a perfect image of the moon, the darkened landscape stretching between, painted grey and black and silver. The bright spots of fires glow orange, several in Edinburgh, the black smoke connecting the earth to the sky. Stars glitter, more than I've ever seen.

"It's beautiful," I say, the words snatched by the wind of our flight.

My hair whips into Hunter's face but he doesn't complain. His arms hold me tight against his body, one hand on my hip, the other curled on my ribs, the heel lightly pressing the side of my breast. I'm pretty sure he can't feel that through my layers. He's only in his shirt, trousers and boots.

I'd be an icicle if that's all I were wearing.

His chest and shoulders ripple with the beat of his wings. So much power in his muscles, the strength of his arms. I hook my toes around his calves to keep my legs from dangling since I don't have washboard abs to fight gravity. Hunter glides over Edinburgh, weaving between columns of smoke and circling the hump of the castle on its hill. My heart jumps at the dark fingers of flats on the skyline.

Is Steph still there, alive and well? What would she think if I rocked up with Hunter? What would anybody think?

Traitor. Whore.

Hardly. Hunter hasn't killed anyone since I rescued him and angel courtship is a little too brutal for me to survive. Hunter would dominate me easily.

Tingles swirl through my belly but since he chooses this moment to swoop low to the ground, I'm pretty sure it's vertigo. I gasp and my fingers tense on his arms. A sound rumbles into my ear.

"Are you laughing at me, Hunter?" I manage to say past the heart flopping around in my mouth.

A couple of heavy beats propel us towards the stars. If I turn my head one way, I can see the shadow of his wing stroking the air. The other way, and there's his face, his eyes the same colour as the sky. They glitter the same, too.

"You wriggle when I do this," he says.

He tucks his wings. Wind roars in my ears. Blackness rushes to greet us. I make an, "Eep!" sound that no heroine in any of my books has ever made in the arms of their monster. I attempt to burrow into Hunter's chest using my spine. He extends his wings and we dip into a curve, gravity tugging at me. Winter-bare trees flash past, their branches white in the dark. We zoom over fields and buildings, the flicker of candle- or torch-light the only sign of people.

There's the noise again. Chuckling.

"You're a bastard," I say when I coax my voice out from hiding.

"Is that good?"

I glower at him. "No."

He grins at me and I tell myself it's his arms crushing my ribs making it hard to breathe. Not that.

"Would you like me to do it again?"

I open my mouth to tell him to go to hell and say, "Okay."

Up we go, until the vastness of the sky swallows the ground. Hunter is an angel gilded in silver. We must be level with the moon.

"Maia?" he says.

"What?"

"Open your eyes."

Dammit.

I glimpse a smile. He twists us into a loop, the world a blur of upside-down black, and we drop. The wind steals my scream. Tingles fizz to my fingers and toes. Or I'm getting frostbite. Excitement and fear war in my stomach, expanding until I'm swollen with them. Every hair stands on end. My heart thunders in my ears.

It's amazing.

I'm still trying to recover when Hunter lands on the roof of Newhailes. He lowers my boots to the tiles. I spin around. My face is numb, my nose is running, my hair is a knotted mess and I'm shaky with adrenaline so my thank-you hug is more of a flop into his arms. He catches my elbows while I headbutt his chest.

"That—that was…"

"Good?"

"*Wonderful.*"

We sit on the peak of the roof and watch the moon. My adrenaline shakes become shivers. I inch closer to Hunter. He doesn't flinch even when I press myself into his side and slide my legs under his. A warm weight rustles over my shoulders and I cuddle into his wing, tucking it around me like a blanket. My thumb brushes the laces running up the side of his leg.

When did I put my hand on his thigh? Maybe he hasn't noticed.

I peek at him from under my lashes. He's watching me, his eyes deep, fathomless black. He holds my gaze and slowly places his hand over mine.

"This is what humans do?"

My chest seems a little tight. Where has all my air gone?

"Not quite," I squeak, and want to slap myself.

"We are not holding hands?"

I flip my hand and tangle my fingers in his. His hand isn't much bigger than mine. Longer, slimmer fingers. My fingertips graze his knuckles.

"Now we are," I say.

He's so warm, I want to climb into his lap and pull him around me like an extra coat. But he may take it the wrong way.

Is there a wrong way?

I should probably let go of his hand. I focus on the moon drifting across the sky, the unbroken stars. Hunter doesn't let go of my hand.

Is he still looking at me? I dare not check.

I guess he's conquered his touch phobia. Or maybe it was a protective mechanism. If no one will touch you except to fight, best not to touch at all.

How lonely.

Do angels get lonely? And what happens when a lonely angel has the chance for contact after years of nothing? Maybe he gets so desperate, so *hungry,* he loses control. We're the only ones here. If he wants something badly enough, he can take it. He's too strong for me to stop him. Would I want to stop him?

Yes, you idiot.

My breathing speeds, white fogging in a cloud around my face. Hunter is silent, still, watchful. His hand is light in mine. He shifts slightly and my heart rockets into my mouth.

My sword is trapped between us. Useless.

Hunter's thumb tickles across my palm. The tiny caress arrows heat between my legs and sends tingles to my fingertips. The same blend of excitement and fear from our flight clenches my stomach.

"We should celebrate!" I squeak.

Again with the squeaking.

"Celebrate what?" Hunter says.

"My first flight!"

I really need to tone it down about twenty decibels.

I jump to my feet and wobble on the peaked roof. My boot slips on ice-rimed tile. Hunter scoops me into his arms before my arse hits the slope, catapulting us off the edge. I squeak for the third—or fifth—time this evening. Hunter's boots thud on the lawn and he bends his knees, hunched over me. His wings brush the frosted grass, leaving swirly patterns that are darker under the moonlight. I stagger a couple of steps to stand alone and pinch my thigh, concentrating on the pain to calm my breathing.

What better way to attract a predator than act the scared, shivering mouse?

"How do we celebrate?" says the predator in question.

"How do angels usually celebrate?"

He gives me his implacable face.

"Right—sex. Of course." I turn my head to stare at the moon and hide my blush.

"How do humans celebrate?" he says.

Is his voice deeper or am I imagining it? I steel myself to

look at him and ignore the flutters when his eyes meet mine.

"We drink," I say.

14

Hunter refuses to let me shop for supplies alone despite the fact we're likely to encounter humans at night, not angels.

"Humans kill each other," he says.

"They'll kill you if they see you."

"They won't see me."

I can't exactly chain him up so he gets to come. Though I do still have the shackles...

He accepts the second iron-forged sword from the library with a sneer of distaste but warriors can't be choosers. He ties the scabbard to the waist of his trousers with the laces he seems so fond of.

I direct him to the Co-Op in Musselburgh for my second flight of the evening. He drops me outside and disappears in a whispering leap. No matter how hard I try, I can't see him in the dark sky.

Inside the shop, the shelves have been picked over since I was last here but I manage to fill my holdall and backpack with more food, toiletries and other essentials. I sneak outside and scan the rooftops for a winged figure. A dog barks in the distance, the only sound in the quiet street. No lights flicker in nearby windows.

Maybe this place was purged.

I shiver and whisper, "Hunter?"

Nothing. I twist my neck to check he's not popped up behind me but the road is empty. I hug the holdall tight to my chest and walk to the corner.

"Hunter?" I say, louder.

Maybe a group of angels came for him. Or a skilled pack of humans set an ambush and he's lying in a gutter in a tangle of frothy silver blood and feathers.

I jog to the next corner. "Hunter!"

"Yes?"

I jump about a foot. The bottles in my backpack clink in protest.

He stands on the edge of a roof, wings slightly spread and silhouetted by the moon. Shadows hide his face but not the glitter of his eyes. I swallow. And again. My heart makes it difficult.

I got a fright. It's not because I was worried about him.

He manages both me and my laden bags with no apparent increase in effort, whisking us all back to the security room at Newhailes in no time.

Okay, so having him along came in handy.

I kick the holdall to the side and pull a bottle from the backpack—coconut rum. Good start.

"Have you ever tasted alcohol?" I say.

Hunter settles himself in the chair. "No."

I blow on my frigid fingers and grin at him. "This'll be fun."

I fill two glasses and hand him one. He sniffs the clear liquid, his eyes narrowed.

"What does it do?"

"Helps you relax."

"Do I need to relax?"

"Desperately," I say, and he tosses me a dark look.

What will a drunk Hunter be like—sleepy, giggly? Nah, probably not. Argumentative? Possibly. Horny? Maybe. This could be another bad idea but my curiosity gets the better of me. And I'm hoping for a talkative Hunter.

Nothing else.

"Let's play a game." I sink into the air mattress and cross my legs. "It's called *Truth or Dare.*"

Hunter gives me a blank stare.

"We each take a turn and decide if we want to tell the truth or do a dare," I say. "If you choose truth, I ask you a question and you have to answer truthfully. If you choose dare, I tell you to do something and you have to do it, and vice versa when it's my turn. You're not allowed to change your mind once you've selected truth or dare though you can pass but you will be punished."

"What is the punishment?"

His intense gaze swoops into my gut.

"Um…" I glance frantically around the room. "You have to down your whole drink."

He sniffs the glass again and takes a sip. His eyes widen.

"It is sweet. I like it."

He swallows the rest and shudders, his feathers rustling.

"Hunter! You're not supposed to down it now. Pace yourself."

I refill his glass and sip my own. The coconut rum glides to warm my belly. I take another mouthful for some courage.

"Okay, you go first—truth or dare?" I say.

He examines my face as if it holds the answer. "Which choice is the greater test?"

"Both, though dare is riskier as you could be asked to do anything."

"Anything?"

"Nothing harmful," I say quickly.

He gulps his drink and raises his chin.

"Dare," he says, his eyes sparking in challenge. Or he's drunk already.

I swallow some rum. I should probably slow down, too, but I need to drown the nerves fizzing in my stomach.

I grin at him. "I dare you to take off your boots."

His brows shoot up. He slurps his drink. A single drop slithers to the line of his jaw. Deft fingers unlace both boots from knee to ankle. It takes about five minutes and I watch, somehow breathless, expecting one or two ailments typical of male feet—hair, finger-length toes—but they're as perfect as the rest of him.

I think the rest of him is perfect? Best not examine that too closely.

His boots thud on the floor. He wiggles his perfect toes and gestures with his glass, clinking it against the bottle and flashing me a triumphant grin.

"Your turn," he says.

I gulp sweet coconut liquid, tempted to chicken out and choose truth.

"Dare," I say.

Hunter leans forward, elbows on his knees. "I dare you to take off—"

He scans me from head to toe. My heart thumps against my ribs. Oh, crap. What if he tells me to take off all my clothes? I'm not drunk enough for this. I warned myself about playing dangerous games—why the hell did I choose *Truth or Dare?*

"—your top," Hunter finishes.

My breath whooshes out and huffs in my glass as I drink

to hide my reaction. The alcohol swirls pleasantly through my brain. Hunter finishes his and swipes the bottle himself. I unzip my hoodie. His eyes track the movement. Thankfully, I'm wearing a t-shirt today, not a vest. My skin tends to prickle under the heat of his gaze.

I toss the hoodie to the side. "Truth or dare?"

"Dare," he says.

He's sprawled in the chair, one wing sticking up, the other trailing to the carpet. He blinks at me but can't seem to coordinate both eyelids.

A drunk Hunter is adorable. Who knew?

"I dare you to keep your eyes closed until it's your turn again," I say.

That should help me get my equilibrium back.

He frowns suspiciously but his eyes slip shut. "What is your choice?"

"Truth," I say.

He cracks one lid to peer at me.

"No peeking!" I say. "Now take your punishment and keep your eyes shut."

He groans and presses his glass to his cheek. I smirk while he drinks.

"Have you kissed someone?" he says, his eyes squinched shut.

I fill his glass and mine, which is also empty somehow, and say, "Yes."

His lashes flutter. His forehead scrunches.

"How many?"

I wag my finger though he can't see. "You only get one question so it's your turn. You can open your eyes."

He spears me with dark midnight-blue. I suck on my drink.

"Truth," he says with another flicker of challenge.

He tips his head to drain his glass and slides bonelessly onto the floor, wings akimbo. His shirt rides up, flashing a flat expanse of stomach and perfectly carved abdominals.

"Am I injured?" he says, his eyes closed once more. "The ground is spinning again."

"You're not injured, you're drunk." I pluck his glass from his limp hand.

He takes a while to focus on me. I sit back on the mattress. He crawls a couple of metres from the base of the wheeled chair and flops beside me, swiping for his glass in my hand. I jerk it out of reach.

"I think you've probably had enough."

He wriggles further onto the mattress. His empty glass clunks on the floor and rolls away. He lurches into a slumped position, his hair flopping over his forehead. His pupils are huge when he looks at me. His warm leg touches mine. And something hard.

"Hunter?"

"Hmm?"

"How many knives do you have on you?"

"Is this my truth question?"

"No," I say.

A smirk slops across his face. "Then seven."

"How?" My eyes follow the long line of his body from chin to toes. Tight shirt, moulded trousers, no boots. "Where?"

"Would you like to search?"

The purr of his voice shivers to low places.

Oh, man. Horny angel, horny me. Alcohol. Bad combination.

I drag my gaze from his before I drown in the darkness. My

supplies line the three walls not taken up by the control desk and screen bank. Hunter's chains are in there somewhere. I meant to detach the stakes for weapons.

"Have you always lived here?" he says. "Before we came?"

An unprompted personal question. This is a first.

"No, it's just a place to hide."

"Why are you alone?"

"I thought it would be safer."

"Alone is safer." He frowns hard. "Except here. I am not alone."

"But you're safe."

He sways closer. Ice and coconut rum and dazed, midnight-blue eyes.

"Safe?" he says, slurring a little.

I take a deep breath to steady myself.

"It wasn't the humans who staked you to the ground, was it, Hunter?"

The question falls into silence. Have I gone too far? If he lashes out in anger, he could snap my neck.

His wings droop.

"No," he says.

"That's what you meant when you told me I made things worse."

He nods and his head bobs for longer than necessary. The air mattress bounces, rocking us together. The floor feels unsteady beneath me.

"I'm sorry," I say.

He raises bleak eyes. "This is war. I am made for it."

"Was it that redhead? The one who doesn't like you?"

"Persipha."

"Not 'Bitch' or 'She-devil'?"

Half of his mouth curves in a smile. "Not to her face."

"Hunter, you made a joke!" I punch him lightly on the shoulder and the half-smile becomes a full-smile. But the humour leaks away and he stares at his hands in his lap.

"She always challenges me."

"To fights?"

"To sex."

"You challenge each other for sex? Why would she do that if she hates you?"

He shrugs one shoulder, bumping against me. "Because she can hurt me."

"How? I thought you were indestructible apart from the iron. That your wounds—what was it?—seal themselves to let you keep fighting."

"It still hurts. It is a test—who can keep fighting with bruises, wounds and broken wings."

"She breaks your wings?"

He tucks his wings into his back. "It is the fastest way to win."

"Can't you say no?"

"The shame of refusal is worse than the shame of losing."

Anger flames in my chest. "That's rape."

"What is rape?"

"Forcing someone to have sex when they don't want to. Is it like that for everyone?"

He drags his gaze from his lap. "No. Persipha is the roughest but the others enjoy the battle. The fights last hours."

"Then the dominant just does what they want? What if you don't like it or it hurts?"

Another shrug. "Do not lose."

"And this is what you endure when you're not hunting?"

A smile ghosts across his face. "At least I am good at hunting."

I pass him the rum bottle. He considers for a second then takes a swig. I swallow a mouthful to calm whatever's going on in my stomach.

"Is that why you're called Hunter?" I say.

"It is the name I was given. The others got to choose."

"Let me guess—there was some kind of fight to determine who got to choose their name and who didn't. Aren't your creators worried about you damaging each other?"

"Sometimes they watch—"

"Jesus Christ."

"—and it forces us to be stronger. Faster. Ruthless. We can heal the damage."

"That's not the point. What about your mental wellbeing?"

"What is mental wellbeing?"

He takes another swig and rolls the bottle between his palms, watching the liquid swirl. I sit on my hands to keep from touching him.

"I think I am defective," he says to the rum.

"You're not defective, Hunter. You're the only sane one."

His throat works as he drinks. I ease the bottle from his grip and put it away.

"But the others rejoice in the battle. They tear and break and bruise. They dominate by force."

He flops on his back, his wings spread flat. His eyes flutter shut.

"I just want to be gentle," he sighs.

I kneel beside him, wobbling on the mattress and careful of his wing. I place a steadying hand on his chest and his heart thuds under my palm. He peers at me from half-lidded eyes.

"You can be gentle," I say. "You liked the hug, didn't you?"

His chin twitches up and down. I brush the hair off his forehead. Black lashes caress his cheeks, his lips half-parted. His pulse flutters in the hollow of his throat.

Vulnerable.

Though he's still intimidating when he's floppy-drunk. All that muscle. The promise of power. Darkness and shadows.

I lean closer, my heart hammering faster than his. His breath tastes of frost and coconut. Alcohol sloshes through my brain and numbs the little voice babbling about inhibitions and impulse control and *should I really be touching him?*

"There are many ways to be gentle," I whisper, and my lips graze his.

Oh, man, they're soft.

I kiss him. He breathes and lies very still.

Too still.

I jerk upright, nerves wriggling through my stomach. His eyes are shut, his breathing deep, muscles relaxed.

Dammit. Way to molest him when he's unconscious. I'd fit right in with the rest of his species. None of them gives a crap about consent.

I rub my mouth with a shaking hand. The warmth of him lingers. The softness. My fingertips trace the curve of his lips and I snatch my hand away. I curl into a ball on the tiny corner of the mattress not taken up by Hunter's sprawled, lightly snoring body.

I'm glad he fell asleep, not disappointed. I do *not* want to snog an angel if that's even what he would have allowed. How would I know? I've just assaulted him. It's the stupid alcohol's fault. Hopefully, Hunter won't remember a thing.

Shame I will.

15

I dream of feathers. They drift from the sky to tickle my skin and I roll around in them. Buck naked. They're warm, so warm, and silky. They touch me everywhere and feel like hands. Strong hands, slim fingers. Ice and tingles. Someone whispers my name, over and over and—

"Maia?"

I gasp awake with his name in my mouth and my name echoing in the security room.

I'm curled on Hunter's wing, nuzzling the feathers. He lies on his back, twisted as much as my weight pinning him will allow. He could have tossed me off in a graceless heap but seems content to watch me.

And there are the tingles.

I scramble off him, my brain thumping, and busy myself with our usual daytime activities: breakfast (for me), tea, exercise, more tea, lunch (for me). I find myself staring at his mouth. The way he blows on his tea. The quirk of a lip when he smirks. A rare smile. I imagine what it would have felt like if he'd kissed me back.

He woke up with no hangover and fuzzy memories of talking about his sexually aggressive—and just plain aggressive—culture. He says he doesn't like the human version of relaxing.

Too much loss of control. The last thing he remembers is saying he was defective.

He asks what happened after that.

I distract him with a movie, the battery on the DVD player critically low despite my careful conservation. *Warm Bodies* probably isn't the best idea, what with a zombie falling in love with a human, but it's my favourite and way more PG13 than the book I've been reading him.

He leans closer to the screen when the characters kiss near the end and the scene reflects in the black of his eyes. The wing nearest me flutters, feathers whispering across my shoulders. Hunter turns his head to look at me. My heart sprouts mini-wings and flaps around its cage of ribs. Light curves on one perfect cheekbone to caress the corner of Hunter's mouth, the rest in shadow.

He's a warrior angel. A *curious* warrior angel from the sword on his hip to his boots that lace to the knee but that doesn't mean he wants to kiss me.

And I shouldn't want to kiss him.

"Would you teach me proper swordplay?" I say in my calmest voice.

He cocks a brow. "Real training requires years of practice."

"I want to be able to defend myself if I bump into an angel." I meet his eyes. "A bad angel."

"I am a good... angel?" he says with only the slightest hitch.

"Well, you've stopped trying to kill me."

He shakes his head. "You cannot fight one of us with a sword."

"Yeah, yeah—resistance is futile. But then, as I'm sure you recall, I stabbed you in the chest."

He scowls. "A fluke."

We clear a space in the library and he teaches me as the sun sets. How to hold the sword in perfect balance, how to move my feet, where to strike. We parry with the scabbards on to avoid accidental disembowelling—of me, not him. His super-healing body would seal all that off before one loop of intestine could graze the floor.

He moves like a shadow in a black blur of power. It's intoxicating. Dark eyes on me, the flash of wings, the clash of sword sheaths. He slips under my guard to press a blunt tip to my stomach, my throat, beneath my breast. He twirls easily behind me to stab me in the back. But every now and again, I block him or dodge or sneak through his guard and get to enjoy the surprise on his face.

"You are not unskilled," he says when we stop.

I flop into a chair and he stands over me, barely breathing hard.

"High praise from a warrior angel."

"But if you meet another," he continues as if I haven't spoken, "do not engage—run."

"Running is also futile, remember?"

"I was being intimidating."

"It worked."

"Yet you stood your ground," he says and there's a hint of something in his voice that blooms warmth in my chest.

I drop my gaze but that doesn't help since I'm eyeball-level with his crotch. The rest of me heats.

I jerk my eyes to his face. "Fancy another night-time adventure?"

"More alcohol?"

"I think it's safer if we avoid that."

"Then where?"

"Home," I say.

16

"This is where you live?" Hunter says over the howl of the wind, circling the black monolith of a building.

A fire burns in the street below, casting orange light on concrete and patchy grass. Rain speckles my face and beads on my lips, sticking my hair to my cheeks.

Our flight is not quite as pleasant as last night.

"Can you see anything?" I say.

He swoops around and spirals downward. Balconies circle each level, giving the flats an almost Japanese look in the dark.

"No," he says. "There is material across the windows."

"Curtains," I say.

He lands at the entrance, setting me down, his eyes always scanning. His hand curls around the hilt of the sword at his hip. I try to lead but he smirks and sweeps me behind him, giving me a faceful of feathers and jostling me with the holdall on his back.

"You're the one at risk from people at night," I grumble, following him up the steps.

He tosses me an arrogant look and turns the first corner.

"They are at risk," he says.

"We're not here to hurt anyone."

"And if they attack?"

"Disarm and show them the error of their ways."

He snorts and pauses to listen, his head cocked. Breathing fills the stairwell—mine and nothing else. The chill nibbles at my skin. My torch glistens on the damp wall, the light muted by my hand cupped around it. Hunter makes no sound as he springs up the stairs and I stomp behind him. He eases through the fifth-storey fire door, scouting the hall between my flat and Steph's.

I wave a hand at him. "Wait here. If she's in there, you're kind of hard to explain."

"You do not want to introduce me to your friend?"

It's hard to read his eyes in the shifting shadows of torchlight. He stands with his feet spread, hand on his sword. Battle ready. He's tall but his presence takes up more of the hallway than height alone. The span of his wings helps. Black in the blackness.

"Maybe another day," I say.

He passes me the holdall and I pull my keyring from my jeans pocket. Two keys. I slot one in and turn the lock. The beam of my torch slices yellow beyond the door, casting humped shadows from Steph's extensive shoe rack.

"Steph?" I whisper, leaving the door open behind me.

I hope I'm not about to scare her if she's sleeping. I hope no one comes bounding up the stairs into the hallway to come face to face with Hunter in the dark.

I feel a little braver knowing he's out there.

A long hall extends past a boiler cupboard, bathroom and bedroom, ending at a glass door into the living room and kitchen. A mirror image of my flat, with more paintings of flowers and extra-wide doors. A vase glitters in the light, something brown and shrivelled drooping over the edge. The air smells of old perfume. No hint of rot.

"Steph?" I say, louder, creeping deeper into the flat.

The sheets on the bed are pristine. An iPod and lamp sit on the bedside cabinet. Her dressing table is one of those ancient ones with chunky bulbs around the border, the polished top completely hidden by bottles and pots and potions.

No one in the bathroom. I push into the living room. Her wheelchair lies on its side in the middle of the carpet.

"Steph!"

I drop the holdall and dart into the kitchen but she's not baking brownies with her headphones in. The counters are wiped clean, a plate and a bowl in the drying rack. Maybe she went for a night-time stroll.

Sure.

"Hunter?"

He appears in the doorway before I can blink and even though I'm expecting it, I jump. Seriously, he gives me heart palpitations.

"Please tell me there's no dust in here." My voice hitches at the end.

I hide my face from his gaze. He drifts through the flat, as silent as a ghost.

"There is no dust," he says.

I blow out a breath. "Then where the hell is she?"

"Perhaps she is staying with another human."

"She doesn't know anyone else."

Hunter shrugs. "It is normal for humans to unite against adversity."

"How do you know so much about us? The knowledge you have would take years of study—language, culture, technology."

"A hunter must know the strengths and weaknesses of their

prey. We are built to know."

I shiver. "Sometimes I forget you're not human then you say something creepy."

"Humans hunt."

"And that's another way we ruined our planet." I walk past him into the hall. "Come on. Let's get out of here."

"You are leaving the supplies?"

"She might come back."

I pull the front door shut and test the lock. Hunter crosses the hallway and places his hand flat on wood.

"This is your home?"

"You want to see? It's nothing special."

This time, he lets me precede him. The place smells stale but the familiarity of the rooms pings in my gut. My bookshelf, TV and PlayStation, the kitchen I barely cooked in, my cosy bed.

I haven't slept in a bed for weeks. The memory-foam mattress calls to me. Hunter can guard me while I nap, right? His blue-black eyes watching me at my most vulnerable.

Probably a bad idea.

He's had several nights to watch me sleep, should he be so inclined.

"All this is yours?" he says, running a finger across the spines of my books.

"Do you not have your own room on your spaceship?"

"No."

"Communal? Yeesh. What about here? Edinburgh Castle has lots of rooms."

He glances at me. "We use a fortified basement."

Well-protected, good vantage point. Just what any invading army needs.

Hunter stalks for the door and the wedge of black beyond. I trail after him into my hall.

"You don't have to go back there," I say quietly. "You can…"

What? Stay with me? His race may be brutal but he's hardly going to abandon them to live on a dying planet.

He stops but doesn't turn around. I tip-toe closer to him.

Is he angry, disgusted? Moved to tears? I wish I knew what he was thinking.

"Someone is coming," he says and his voice gives me nothing. "Steph?"

"Several humans."

"Oh. Hide?"

I ease the front door shut, wincing at the click of the lock. I open the boiler cupboard and motion Hunter inside. He crowds me, herding me in first, his back to the door. I wedge myself between the cold metal boiler and the wall. It's a tight fit with Hunter and his wings. I thumb my torch off, plunging the tiny space into blackness. My pulse kicks. Muffled voices mumble through the wall. The fire door slams. Footsteps slap on stairs, fading to the background noise of my heartbeat.

I can't see Hunter but the heat and icy scent of him are dizzying in the cramped cupboard. I feel the weight of his eyes on me.

I clear my throat. "I meant what I said. You don't need to go back to the people who abused you."

He says nothing and I babble some more, whispering to the dark.

"You don't fit in. But you can be what you want here. You know, when the rest of your people stop murdering us and bugger off."

My eyes ping-pong, struggling for some hint of Hunter in

the unrelieved blackness.

"I'm only saying this because of what you said when you were a little tipsy on the rum."

Why am I telling him this? I really should shut my mouth.

Feathers rustle. My heart speeds.

"What did I say?"

His soft voice bleeds from the dark and raises goosebumps on my arms. I cuddle the torch to my chest, not caring if I look ridiculous to Hunter with his perfect, night-penetrating eyeballs.

"You..." I lick my lips. Jeez, he's so intimidating, even when I can't see him. "You said you wanted to be gentle."

"I am not gentle," he says stiffly.

I roll my eyes, forgetting he can see me. "You can still be a badass and be gentle, Hunter. They're not mutually exclusive."

I fumble for the switch on the handle of the torch, needing to see his face, see if he's sneering at me. He plucks the torch from my grip.

"Hey!" I hiss. "Fine, you don't want to be gentle. What exactly do you want, oh moody warrior angel?"

Silence stretches from seconds into minutes. I shuffle my feet and force myself to stop.

Has he gone, slipped out somehow? Seeped through the cracks in the door like black fog?

My hand itches to reach out but I'm afraid of what will happen if I touch him.

"What do you want, Hunter?" I say minus the mocking tone.

"Take off your clothes," he says.

17

Several appropriate responses run through my head:

"Presumptuous, much?"

"You first."

A good slap, though I'd probably miss.

"All of them?" I squeak instead.

Hunter's presence fills the cupboard and makes it difficult to breathe. My palms start sweating.

This is madness. He can't think I'll just take off my clothes because he says so—

Why am I unzipping my jacket?!

The heavy material scrapes the wall and flops to my boots. It takes two shaky attempts to tug my hoodie and t-shirt off in a oner instead of unzipping one and pulling off the other and delaying what appears to be the inevitable. Chill air caresses exposed skin.

I must look ridiculous—cheap Marks & Spencer bra that's been washed too many times, tangled hair frizzed by the rain. Wide eyes, dilated pupils. Mouth breathing.

I unbutton my jeans and slide the zip down, the sound unbearably loud in the dark. I chicken out from going further—my pink polka dot pants really don't match the white bra—and reach for Hunter. My hands brush something solid.

I pop one button on his shirt and spread the collar, warm muscle under my palms. Fingers manacle my wrists, pinning both hands and bending my arms to the side. My knuckles ring softly on the boiler. I swallow hard, the position twisting my shoulder but hiding my breasts at least.

"Hunter?" I say and my voice wobbles.

There's a light touch on my cheek. I shut my eyes but there's no difference between the darkness of my lids and the darkness of the cupboard. The touch loops over my forehead, down the other cheek and strokes my jaw. It traces my mouth. I kiss the exploring finger and the touch disappears. Hunter forces my hands high, above my head, pressing me to the wall.

Now that's not fair.

The touch returns to my face, my jaw. A hand curls around my throat. My pulse thuds against the pressure.

He could kill me so easily, is that what he's implying? We're alone in the flat. I'm trapped in a cupboard with a dangerous creature. I should let him do what he wants.

The hand slides down to trace each collarbone and dip into the hollow between. My pulse jumps against his finger.

What is he doing? Is he enjoying it? Am *I*? Being manhandled by a horny, arrogant angel who thinks he can just do what he wants...

Why did I encourage him to do what he wants?

His hand draws a line between my breasts. Since I've not got much to shout about in the boob department, his finger barely grazes them and skips over the underwire of my bra.

Is he disappointed? Female angels have bodies as perfect as their faces and no lack of womanly curves. I'm a starving teenage boy compared to them.

A finger circles my bellybutton and I bite my lip. It's as if the circling caress is lower, circling my most delicate part—

Oh, boy. I guess I am enjoying it.

His hand explores my ribs, breasts, stomach. He tugs me off the wall and follows the cleft of my spine until his fingers cradle the back of my head.

Only his hands touch me—two scalding points of contact in the dark. Every sense is tuned to them while I'm blind, waiting. Aching. The thrill of being helpless, the anticipation, the danger. The cold metal of the boiler, the heat of Hunter. My confused body swings between flushed and shivering.

It's the most erotic thing I've ever done.

Though I'm not exactly a lady of experience. My first boyfriend was far too excited at the thought of deflowering a rebellious Catholic girl. It was over so quickly, it was like he was the virgin. The other was snide and pasty.

And I've had a long, *long* period of sexual inactivity since then.

Hunter pushes me back to the wall. His hand splays on my belly. His fingers dip into my jeans, over my underwear, which—let's face it—is sodden. The hand jerks away.

He really needs to stop that.

I clamp my teeth on a whine. I strain to see him, hear him, touch him but his grip is iron on my wrists, though not painful. Just enough to know I can't get away.

Who does he think he is, pawing at me, teasing me? No doubt smirking in the blackness.

But I really want him to put his hand in my pants.

Fingers cup between my legs, skin to skin. A moan flutters to the ceiling on butterfly wings but there are hundreds left over to buzz in my stomach. The hand moves and—oh, sweet lord—a slim finger glides back and forth. My knees buckle but his hand on my wrists keeps me in place. Muscles tremble. I'm throbbing everywhere he touches, everywhere he's touched.

I try not to think what I look like to him—half-naked, sagged against the wall, legs spread, face slack in some awful lusty expression.

The finger slides inside me.

Holy freaking hell, I'm close already.

My body clenches around him, sensitised by his hand, by the deprivation of everything but him. His thumb circles the nub at my apex, his finger gliding in and out and oh *fuck* it feels amazing.

How is he good at this?

I can't help it—I thrust my hips against his hand, driving his finger deeper, harder inside me.

So close, so close, *so close.* The orgasm rushes towards me, fizzing in my veins, swelling outward from the press of his hand. I sob his name.

The hands vanish at the last second, taking my climax with them. My arse hits the floor and I blink at nothing, sprawled in my discarded clothes.

"We have to go," Hunter says, his voice exactly the same.

No hint of strain or heat or hunger.

My mouth flaps. "What? I'm... What?"

The door opens and a slice of lighter blackness silhouettes him. I scrabble into my clothes, my skin prickling. Humiliated tears spring to my eyes. I stomp out of the cupboard to where he's waiting in the hall between my flat and Steph's.

I suck in a breath. "What is your—"

He tosses me over his shoulder and bounds down the stairs. For a second, I'm stunned and hang limp, jiggling on top of his wing. The outer door swings. Rain splatters icy needles on my back where my jacket has bunched up.

"Hunter!" I hiss, and wriggle in his arms. "Put me down."

I squirm and shove at his shoulder. His arm loosens. I slide down the very solid front of him and stumble a couple of steps on wobbly legs.

He's perfectly calm, his face betraying nothing, while I'm a panting mess with hair tangled over my cheeks.

"What was... You can't just... Why didn't you..."

The only thing I really want to say is, "Couldn't you have let me finish?"

The unsatisfied ache is distracting. My skin tingles, for goodness' sake. Maybe it's the embarrassment and not the ghost of his hand caressing my body.

He watches me pace, my fingers fisted in my hair. The rain helps cool my flush.

I could make an excuse—I need some space, some air—and ditch him, disappearing into the streets. Would serve him right.

Who am I kidding? His bloody name is Hunter. He'll find me in a second.

And I like our little nook at Newhailes.

"You do not want me?" he says, his eyes black and unreadable.

I stop. Frown at him. Slow my breathing.

"No, that's—"

He launches himself at me.

I have one second to regret starting my sentence with 'no'.

18

I forget the sword in my belt, and duck as if that will save me from sixty kilos of enraged angel.

But Hunter soars over me, the tips of his feathers tickling the hands covering my head. I peek through my fingers. He lands in a crouch, wings huge and spread to their fullest. The slits in his shirt flash glimpses of smooth back.

Then I hear the singing.

Hunter's shoulder jerks. He yanks an arrow into his hand and snaps it in two. His blade scrapes from its ancient sheath.

"Run, Maia," he says.

Another arrow wails towards us from the dark and rain beyond the burning vehicle. Hunter swipes it away with his sword. The eerie blue twirls into the soaked grass.

"I can help—"

He twists his head to glare at me through the hair fallen over his forehead, both hands clasping the sword in front of his face.

"*Run*," he growls.

I sprint for the corner of the building, not wanting to draw the angels inside. I throw myself behind a stinking, metal skip and draw my sword.

Why are angels attacking at night? That's not fair.

I slide along rusting metal, my nose buried in my elbow to mask the stench of uncollected rubbish slowly rotting. I crawl into a black alcove created by a narrow but thick wooden door canted against the skip. Stones bite into my knuckles.

Five angels surround Hunter near the flaming car, firelight haloing the white-gold of their wings. Blue swords deaden the cold beauty of their faces. They mock him in their language while he stands alone. A sword slices down. Metal rings on metal. Six angels launch into the air. The battle is like nothing I've ever seen—speed, grace, the beat of wings and the clash of blades.

Human resistance is laughable compared to this display of power. How I managed to stab Hunter in the first place is a mystery. He's amazing, swooping and twirling in the sky, his wings part of his defence as they sweep through his attackers, blocking their blows and knocking them aside.

How can he be the weakest when he fights like this?

Surprise registers on more than one perfect face.

They hurt him before. Bruised, bled, broke his wings. But now he has an iron sword.

Silver blood arcs onto the grass. A body crumples in a puff of stained feathers.

Angels fight in terrifying silence, the same silence they use to hunt. The only sounds are the clang of metal and the slap of flesh on flesh, a grunt when a hit slams home. A female flees into the sky in the blackness beyond the fire.

Not Persipha, the bitch.

Three males harry Hunter, blades slicing clothes or clashing on his sword. They retreat for a beat, wings flapping, shoulders heaving. A streak of white stoops from the heavens and tackles Hunter, driving him backwards. They crunch into the burning car and the flames leap higher, engulfing them. Hunter's sword clatters on concrete in the gap between the vehicle and the pavement.

I swallow a gasp of his name and jump to my feet, banging my head on wood. The door topples and I grab it before it hits the ground.

Solid oak. Some kind of wardrobe with a handle in the centre, chunks of wood missing where the hinges would be. Taller than me, but most things are. I heft it in my grip. Not a bad shield.

Hunter won't be debilitated by the fire, I know that. He told me his skin is heat resistant—another fancy attribute added by his creators. He could wrestle with the female for hours in the flames and be fine. Hurt, not maimed. But if one of the others picks up the iron sword then my semi-invincible warrior angel is dead.

Mine? Oh, boy. I've adopted an angel.

Worry about that later.

I gulp a breath of damp air and charge around the corner. Time to say something legendary and heroic.

"Hey, arseholes!" I yell. "Come and get me."

Okay, so it needs some work.

Wings swirl in smoke and flame, obscuring the struggle of Hunter and the female. Three pairs of cold, blank eyes fix on me. A wailing rises in the night and my stomach flips. I swing my shield and two arrows thunk into wood, the tips piercing through to wink at me. I gag and press my sword hand to my mouth, wary of the blade. Sweat pops on my rain-slick forehead.

"You missed, you dick," I croak.

An angel swoops towards me. The female catapults out of

the flames like a comet and tumbles along the road. Hunter rolls off the car and stands with sword in hand. Sparks fly from his black wings, wisps of smoke curling from what's left of his shirt.

The enemy angel charges me, his weapon painting an arc of blue. I yelp and toss my shield up. The blade wedges in the top edge, the force nearly tearing the handle from my grip. The male tugs and I stumble towards him. The wind from his wings chills my wet clothes. He flaps, dragging me up, teetering on tip-toe. I pull with my whole weight on the handle, my weapon raised, and the angel dips. It's more accident than deliberate when my sword skewers his chest.

Thank you, gravity.

Pale eyes widen. A rattle, not unlike the one Hunter made, shivers out of the angel. His eyes roll, his wings fold and he flops on top of me, driving my blade deeper. My back hits the grass and the pommel of my sword punches my solar plexus, disappearing all my air in a painful whoosh.

Screw you, gravity.

I buck and flail on the ground, relearning how to breathe. My shield lies out of reach, knocked from my hand. My sword sticks from the angel's back like a bloody fin, silver in the night. His forehead lolls on the grass and his shoulder is practically up my nose, his scent like wet newspaper, not the fresh, clean smell of Hunter. I shove at the carcass and he shifts. My diaphragm weeps with relief as my hilt lifts clear.

At least the bastard is light. If he had the human weight of all that muscle, I'd be suffocating right now.

His body turns to lead. The leverage I gained thuds him into me and awards me with another bruising blow to the solar plexus. Tears spring to my eyes. I wheeze and blink them away.

What the fuck, gravity?

Another angel looms into my line of sight, a chilling smile on his thin lips. He braces his foot on the dead angel's spine and leans closer. The pommel of my sword attempts to burrow into my intestines. Rain, tinged orange by firelight, streaks past white-gold wings.

"Human," he says, his voice emptier than his eyes, "I get you."

He raises his bow. Muscles flex and the blue tip of an arrow aims for my eyeball.

19

I jerk my head to the side, as if the outcome will be different should the arrow enter my temple instead of my eye.

Hunter fights the two remaining angels, the female on his back and clawing at his face while the male batters him with his sword. Metal clashes in a constant stream of noise. He seems to look at me but the male blocks him, his assault unrelenting.

"Hunter will not help you, human," the angel above me says.

His dead comrade bleeds on my jacket, warm on my hand where I grip the hilt, trying and failing to relieve the crushing pressure. His acidic blood tingles where it touches skin. I force myself to meet the angel's gaze instead of looking at Hunter, willing him to break free and save me.

"You couple, yes? Humans are the only thing he can dominate. Weak."

"He's not weak," I wheeze. "You lot are a bunch of psychopaths."

Something dark stirs in the angel's eyes and makes me wish for the emptiness of before. Whatever he's thinking, it's terrifying.

"Shame for you to not dominate him," he says. "Hunter is good on his knees."

Bile squirts into my throat and nearly drowns me. I slowly,

slowly, bend my leg, bringing my boot closer to my free hand.

"You raped him?" I say and the words burn my tongue.

The angel cocks his head. The familiar gesture aches in my chest.

Hunter does it all the time.

"What is raped?" the angel says.

Heat flares in my knee, thigh and hip as I twist my body as little as possible. My fingers strain across the freezing grass.

"Taking what isn't yours," I say through gritted teeth.

"He lost. He was mine to take."

Breathing digs the pommel of my sword deeper into my skin despite the layers of my jacket and hoodie. The angel relaxes the string of his bow, the arrow pointing to the side.

"Perhaps I should take you, human. You would not survive long." He glances towards the sound of fighting. "Pity. No time."

The bow stretches taut. Blue light swirls from the tip of the arrow and seems to sink into my eyeball, roiling with my stomach contents.

I hope pretty flowers grow from my dust.

The arrow starts to hum. My gut cartwheels, taking my heart with it. I lunge for my boot. Stinging fingers snatch the dagger, the one used to carve Hunter when his own people pinned him like a butterfly.

The angel breathes out.

I stab the dagger into his calf.

And keep stabbing, hacking at soft flesh. His shrieks smother the song of the arrow. It thwacks into the ground next to my head. The angel launches skyward, howling what I presume are obscenities. Hot liquid splatters my face.

"Filthy human!" he screams, and nocks a second arrow.

He disappears in a streak of black and smoke. I blink at the sky, water filling my eyes.

Rain, of course. Angel-killing heroes don't cry.

"Jesus," I say and my voice wobbles. "Jesus-holy-mothering-*Christ.*"

I try to move but the arrow has pierced my jacket at the shoulder and the fletching at the end tangles in the material. I shove at the body on top of me and it flops to the side, taking my sword with it but blocking me from the sight of any angels in that direction. My solar plexus weeps in gratitude.

I try to sit up, rip myself free, but the shaft is sunk deep in the hard ground. The arrow swirls blue from the corner of my eye. Nausea scoops out my stomach and propels everything into my mouth. I clamp my lips and grab the slick, cold shaft. A freezing jolt shocks my arm. I whimper and cradle my hand to my chest.

Pinned, like Hunter, helplessly waiting for someone to find him. Knowing the outcome would be the same whether it be angel or human—both would see him dead.

Except this human.

I grip the dagger in my fist and wait. Feathers rustle. A shape eclipses me. Dark hair, dark eyes. Wings as black as the sky. Hunter crouches over me on all fours.

"Are you hurt? Did it taste skin?"

He thrusts onto his knees, freeing his hands, which hover over me. His wings arch and muffle the rain. I shake my head.

"Just my jacket," I say, "though that's not alive so I guess it doesn't count."

My brave laugh dissolves into a sob. I hide my face in my sleeve, soaked with mud, dirt, blood, probably some sludge from the skip. A sharp tug frees my clothes. Gentle hands hold me against a solid, wonderfully warm chest.

Wow, the fire really didn't spare much of his shirt.

I cuddle into him, my fingers sliding around his smooth back. I may sniff him a little—ice with a hint of ash and metal.

"We should go," he says after a couple of minutes. "Angels hunting at night means they are desperate."

"Hey, you said angels without a hitch."

"Too much time around humans."

His smirk squiggles into my chest. I wipe my nose on my sleeve, like a lady, and climb to my feet, tucking the dagger in my boot. My gaze falls to the skewered angel. Hunter braces his foot on the corpse's shoulder and yanks my sword free. I squeeze the hilt in my hand, comforted by the weight.

"It was a good kill," Hunter says.

"My first kill."

"You bled another."

"I didn't like him."

Hunter stares off to the edge of the grass. Feathers waver in the branches of a decorative shrub. The angel is in more pieces than when I last saw him.

"I did not like him either," Hunter says.

The other three bodies lie near the burning car. Firelight dances in pools of silver.

"Well, in our tally for the night, you get four and I get one," I say, my voice light. "That means you win."

Hunter pivots slowly, his black eyes intense.

"I win?"

Oh, crap. In angel rules, that means he gets what he wants. The last time he got what he wanted, he made me strip and pressed me against a wall.

"Um…" I say.

He cocks his head and I want to hug him again but he stays out of reach.

Maybe he still thinks I don't want him. Is he blind?

I open my mouth. Hunter tenses, looking over my shoulder. I start to turn.

"Touch her and die, arsehole," a familiar voice says.

20

A ragged group of ten humans—sorry, *people*—gathers at the front entrance of the block of flats. The leader leans heavily on a bedazzled cane, her raincoat bright pink with a fluffy hood.

"Steph!"

I sheath my sword and wrap my arms around her thin frame. She smells the same—Parma Violets and jasmine.

"I went to your flat. Your wheelchair was knocked over. I thought—"

"Sorry, I was a couple of floors down."

"What happened to the weepers and wailers?"

"Dusted about a week after you left. Got a few others. The rest of us hid. Turns out angels suck at hide and seek." She sweeps me behind her and raises her voice. "What are you staring at, arsehole? Get out of here if you don't want to end up like your friends."

"Yeah, dickhead," a man chimes in, "where are your fancy soul-sucking weapons now?"

I peek around Steph's shoulder. Hunter's hand clenches on the sword hilt at his hip, his wings slightly spread. Ready and wary. Wet hair flops over his eyes and sticks to his cheekbones. Soot and blood smear his face, his chest.

Funny, I didn't notice that before.

One shirt sleeve remains, detached from the collar and crumpled towards his elbow. A flap of material covers one nipple. His other arm is bare apart from the cuff, burnt at the edges.

He looks like an abused Chippendale.

I ease from behind Steph and put myself between her and Hunter. His laced trousers and boots are unmarred from the fire, as flame retardant as their owner.

"Maia, what are you doing?" Steph says, her knuckles white on her cane.

"He's not the enemy. He's different—"

"She's fucking it," the same man says.

I recognise him from one of the upper storeys. Long hair, tattoo of a spiderweb on his hand, always smells of weed. Carl? Craig?

"I'm not fu…"—nope, can't do it—"having sex with him."

Yet, whispers a little voice.

Best not to bring that up.

Steph's hand clamps my chin and raises my head. "Has he brainwashed you? Blink twice if he's holding you against your will."

I stare at her, unblinking, until she releases her grip. The people behind her shuffle and mutter.

"I'm not brainwashed. He's my"—friend? Adopted pet? Potential lover?—"ally," I finish lamely.

Hunter watches us, his arrogant expression in place.

"Oh, Maia," Steph says, "what did I tell you about real life and fantasy? He's not a misunderstood monster who just wants someone to take care of him."

My cheeks flush, cooled quickly by the rain. My damp hair curls down my back, heavy and wet.

"He's not a monster. And, while I appreciate the rescue, what exactly were you going to do if he turned hostile? Is that all the iron and rusted weapons you could find?"

Steph appears unarmed, the rest of her group clutching an assortment of chisels, a poker and a drain pipe. One man has a skillet. Carl/Craig has a chain with a rusted hook on the end. He keeps swinging it around like an old-timey street thug.

"Pickings were slim," Steph says. "And I thought you were in trouble."

I toss her a grin and hold out my fist. "You've always got my back."

"Damn right I do," she says, and bumps me.

I pull the dagger from my boot. "Take this instead. More effective the next time you want to rescue a damsel in distress."

She wraps her fingers around the hilt, her nails perfectly varnished. Beneath her hood, her make-up is pristine. I definitely have soot and more painted on my face.

Probably a lot more after cuddling Hunter.

Steph examines the blade. Pale hair curls around her cheeks. Possibly blonde, possibly pink. In one move, she flicks the dagger at Hunter. He doesn't flinch as it sails past to skitter on the concrete. The corner of his mouth twitches.

"Steph!" I gasp. "What the hell?"

"He really is quite implacable, isn't he?" she says, ignoring my furious flapping. "Does he speak and understand English? Or is he just a pretty keepsake?"

"He's not an object. He speaks."

She limps closer. I dance backwards, trying to keep myself between them.

"Speak then, mighty angel overlord. If you're not going to kill her, what exactly are you going to do?"

I pinch the bridge of my nose. "You did not just ask him about his intentions."

She slips past me while I'm marvelling at her audacity. And she was the one who told me to be careful. Now she's taunting my angel.

An angel. Not mine.

She pokes her manicured nail into the pec modestly covered by a wisp of shirt. My mouth drops open. Not from her brazenness but more that Hunter lets her do it. He could stop her, snap her into little bits, if he wanted to.

"You may be a creature from another universe so let me school you on what you have here," Steph says while I watch, half-fascinated, half-terrified for her life.

Will Hunter strike her if she pisses him off? I'm pretty sure I've pissed him off eighty percent of the time we've been together and he's never raised a hand to me.

"She is my best friend," Steph says, removing her finger long enough to point at me before she pokes it back in his chest. "She is kind, generous. Sometimes too generous. Sweetly naive—"

"Hey, I'm not—"

"—*especially* when it comes to wounded creatures she thinks she can save. You're the one she stabbed in the video, aren't you?"

Hunter raises his dark gaze from the finger prodding his pec to Steph's face. They're the same height, though she's slimmer.

"Yes," he says.

It seems like a while since I heard his voice. Soft, low. Vibrating in places it shouldn't. Steph appears a little stunned herself.

She shakes her head. "Well, don't you dare take advantage of her bleeding heart."

"Oh, come on. I'm no bleeding—"

"She'll have a romanticised notion in her head of how things will go—she'll tame you, you'll fall—"

"Steph, that is ridic—"

"But if you're pretending, if you're really just a monster, you'll leave her the hell alone." Another prod and she gets in his face. "If you hurt her, so help me god, I'll hunt you down and rip off your wings, you overgrown fruit fly."

"Okay," I say, my voice wobbling between mortification and awe, "I think that's enough poking for one night."

I insert myself between them, Hunter huge and warm behind me, Steph shivering in her thin jacket. She taps a couple of steps away and sags on her cane. I lean against the solidity of Hunter then force myself clear when I realise what I'm doing.

"I do not plan on hurting her," he says quietly.

Steph relaxes at whatever she sees on his face. I will myself not to look.

Gentle. He wants to be gentle.

Oh, boy.

"Why are we talking to it?" Carl/Craig huffs, rain spitting from his lips. "Let's just kill it."

Agreement rumbles in the crowd.

My hand tightens on my sword. "No one touches him."

"See—she's fucking it."

"Shut up, Craig or Carl or whatever your name is."

"It's Greg."

"Oh. Well... Shut up, Greg."

"Maia's right," Steph says, addressing the group. "About Greg shutting up and the angel. He's different."

Greg pouts but stops swinging his chain. The rest of the group look disappointed.

She touches my arm. "You're safe with him?"

I glance at Hunter. Black eyes meet mine through a cage of hair.

Could he be any more gorgeous and intimidating?

"Very," I say.

Something flashes across his face and I remember telling him he was safe with me when he was drunk. I keep him safe, he keeps me safe. Though what I want to do to him—and him to do to me—feels anything but safe.

His gaze is too intense for me to hold. I cough and focus on Steph.

"Get the dagger. Keep it close. I left a bag of stuff in your flat."

"Maia, you didn't have to—"

"I've got plenty. Hunter doesn't use much."

"His name is Hunter? Who are his best friends—Assassin and Killer?"

We grin and share a fist bump. Man, I've missed her.

"I'll try and visit every few days," I say, and hug her, "you crazy, wonderful bitch."

She laughs into my hair and whispers, "I'm not the one with a pet angel. Be careful."

I sidle next to Hunter. He seems warier than usual. There's a lot going on in those dark, mysterious eyes.

"Ready to go home?" I say, very close to a squeak.

"I thought this was your home."

"I mean our home."

His gaze attempts to dissect me through my eyeballs and leaves me woozy.

"Our home?" he says.

I turn my back, not entirely sure what's happening with my

expression. Steph and her rabble observe our every move. I give her what I hope is a confident smile when really I have no idea what the hell I'm doing.

"Our home," I say.

Arms wrap around me, thankfully avoiding the throbbing around my midriff where the pommel slammed into me. Wings snap straight, scattering a hail of raindrops. Muscles bunch and tense. Steph seems fascinated but the others wrinkle their noses in distaste.

Their loss.

Hunter launches skyward and my stomach stays on the ground with Steph. The burning car dwindles to an orange blob. Wind and water swirl into my face. The heavy beat of wings thuds like my heart.

"That is best friends?" Hunter says in my ear.

I twist my head enough to smile at him. His mouth grazes my cheekbone. My pulse flaps harder.

"That's best friends," I sigh.

21

"Weird night, huh?" I say to break the silence, flicking on a solar lamp and touching a match to a couple of candles.

Locking the door kicks my heart rate up a notch. The security room is cramped—though nowhere near as bad as the boiler cupboard—and Hunter makes it hard to breathe.

Does he want to pick up where we left off? Should I douse the lights, strip off my clothes and let him do what he wants? He could play with me for hours. *Days*.

I wobble over to my supply stash and rummage around, coming up with wet wipes. The packet crinkles in my shaky hands. I feign nonchalance and flap a wipe at Hunter.

"Here. Use this to clean up. You're covered in soot and the other angels' blood."

He takes and sniffs the wipe with his usual suspicion. He dabs at his cheek. I shrug off my soaked jacket, silvery stains highlighting the blood. A small hole mars the shoulder where the arrow pierced. Damp patches circle my hoodie at the collar and cuffs. A triangle of my t-shirt sticks past the hem. I tug on it and the whole t-shirt comes out in my hand.

I clear my throat. "I, uh, guess I dressed a bit hastily."

At least I noticed before I unzipped my hoodie and exposed myself to Hunter. Though he's seen it already.

His gaze rises from the t-shirt in my fist to my face, lingering in between. My skin flushes in its wake. I pull a wipe from the pack and hide behind it, scrubbing my forehead. It's a good excuse to shut my eyes and give myself a break from Hunter's watchful, intimidating figure.

Why isn't he saying anything?

"Just, um, for clarification," I say, inhaling lime and mint, "I didn't mean 'no.'"

Silence from Hunter. I keep the flimsy shield of the wipe draped over my face.

"To your question," I continue and want to slap myself.

Seriously, if the guy wants to hear me babble stupid crap, all he has to do is stay quiet and my anxiety will do the rest.

"What question?" he says, and I jump.

The wipe flutters to the floor.

Damn. I have to look at him.

The smirk tells me he knows perfectly well what question. The bastard.

I clear my throat again. "You asked if I wanted you."

"And you did not mean 'no'?"

"Right."

"What did you mean?"

Oh, come on.

He palms the wipe over his chest and circles it down to his belly, leaving a clean, glistening path. My tongue suddenly seems too big for my mouth. His fingers dip below the waistband of his trousers, though there's definitely no soot there. But he should take them off, just to be sure.

Oh, crap.

He stops and looks at me. Have I been staring? Drooling?

"I meant I do... Or I don't not... Um..."

What the hell does 'don't not' mean? Why am I tongue-tied like I'm thirteen and he's the most popular boy in school? He's not even from this universe, for Christ's—for goodness' sake.

His wipe drifts to the carpet. Slim, strong fingers tug the remnants of his shirt off with the same sound, I imagine, as a man ripping off a woman's panties in the throes of passion. Hunter plucks another wipe from the packet forgotten in my hand. Instead of moving away, he stays close, his eyes unwavering and sending tingles to my stomach.

"What do you mean, Maia?" he says.

I snatch the wipe from his fingers.

"I think your front is clean," I squeak. "Let me do your back."

I duck around him, comfortable with the illusion that I'm in control when we both know he can do what he wants. Tackle me, pin me to the floor. Or lay me on the air mattress and make love to me all night.

Right. Because angels know how to make love.

I've never been fucked. Thinking about it makes me want to sit down and put my head between my knees until the world doesn't quiver quite so much. Sex with my two (okay, fairly pathetic) boyfriends was sedate. Nice sometimes, I guess. But I've never had tear-off-your-clothes, tooth-and-claw, hot, animal sex. It's got to feel great, right?

Unless it strays into angel coupling territory and tears more than my clothes.

Hunter braces his hands on the wall and bows his head. The slide of muscle in his shoulders distracts me from the edge of a panic attack. His wings spread, giving me room. He has the most beautiful back, even streaked with soot. I touch the cool wipe to warm skin and am rewarded with the tiniest of shivers. My hand swirls across him, separated by a scrap of nothing. It reminds me of the cupboard. His hand in the dark.

My turn to shiver.

I grab the opportunity to explore. Broad shoulders, the swell of ribs, the knobs of his spine dipping into the cleft of his lower back. His trousers sit low. Super low. I bite my lip.

He has butt dimples.

I polish them with the wipe and feel a little faint. I really should stop now. The wipe is filthy. His skin sparkles.

Screw it. He killed four of his own kind, saved my life and didn't hurt Steph when she got protective.

He's been good.

I step into him and press my face between his shoulder blades, inhaling ice, mint and lime. He smells like a virgin mojito and it takes a ridiculous amount of willpower not to lick him. My hands slip around his sides to rest on his chest and the bunch of his perfect abs. He stills. No breathing. He may be an implacable warrior but his heart races under my ear and gives my confidence a boost.

"I want you," I murmur to his back. "That's what I mean. But... I have no idea what you want."

Tension eases from his shoulders. His wings flop over me like a warm, ticklish cloak. His hands cover mine and, just like that, I'm pinned.

"No idea?" he says, his voice a deep purr that blooms heat in low places.

Places recently touched.

I lick my lips and may accidentally lick him, too.

"Some idea," I say. "So why did you stop?"

He slides my hands down silken skin, my fingertips grazing hip bones and the line of his trousers. I command myself not to squirm against his arse.

"I wanted you safe. Here. I was not going to sex you in a cupboard."

My lips curve against his back.

Sex me. How cute.

"Are you laughing at me, Maia?"

"Nope," I say.

One second, I'm snuggling him, the next, he has my arms cuffed behind me, manacled in his fingers. Unlike in the cupboard, he presses me to the front of his body and I'm suddenly at risk of spontaneous combustion. He is solid muscle, heat and hard... um... edges.

So hard.

He shudders at my yelp. His eyes are drowning midnight-black. Everything I wanted in the cupboard.

Maybe this was why he cut things short. He couldn't control himself if we went further. That is freaking sexy.

And terrifying. If he loses control, he could crush my bones. Or kill me.

His fingers skim my cheek, his thumb tracing my bottom lip. My eyes are a little wide, my breathing a little fast. He smiles a rare smile and lowers his mouth to mine. And, since angels don't kiss and his frame of reference is one movie and a painting, it's all he does. Unbearably soft lips. Not moving.

So cute.

I kiss him back. His wings flare in his endearing startle response. His grip loosens on my wrists. I wriggle free and balance on tip-toes, my fingers buried in his hair, my hips arched into him. His height is uncomfortable on my spine but the rest of me doesn't give two craps. I feast on his mouth.

Oh, man, his mouth. Warrior angels learn fast.

He matches my somewhat frantic pace while I attempt to

climb inside him. I'm making small begging noises and can't stop. His hands fall to my hips. His fingers tighten. I slip him some tongue and he trips on my feet, or his feet, and we tumble onto the chair with enough force to roll it into the nearest pile of supplies. Something cracks. Metal clatters. The seat squeals in protest.

I snog Hunter like he's oxygen and I can't suck him down fast enough. I'm in his lap. Sweet mother, I'm *writhing* in his lap and even through my jeans, I'm daunted. But I still want to unwrap him from his trousers and put him in my throbbing places. Maybe I need to slow down. This is his first kiss and I'm humping him like a manic rabbit.

I guess it's *my* control we need to worry about.

I pull away and we pant at each other. His eyes are more dazed than when he was drunk, his hair tousled over flushed cheeks. Both wings stick straight up in soft surprise.

"This is kissing?" he says, and blinks at me. "I want more kissing."

I nibble his lips, suck hard. His tongue meets mine and jolts my pulse. His fingers stay on my hips. I rub myself against his lap.

"Other angels are stupid," he moans in my mouth.

My hands explore the curve of his shoulders, pet his wings, the planes of his chest. I touch him like he touched me in the cupboard and crave more, my skin sensitised by what he started. I need his hands on me. Inside me. Or a finger is fine. Hands would be a bit much.

I'll have to work up to the bulge in his pants.

I break the kiss and immediately want to kiss him again, though I'm dizzy. I kiss his throat. His pulse throbs, echoing mine, which is happily juddering everywhere, even my tongue.

I've never been more aware of my heartbeat, my blood-flushed skin. I move to Hunter's collarbone and trace it with my lips.

Other women may fantasise about biceps, abs or a nice, tight arse but the collarbone is where it's at. It's so vulnerable.

I force myself onward, slithering between Hunter's legs to kneel on the floor. His breath catches when I lick one nipple then the other and dip my head to his stomach. I lose myself for a while in the sensation of silk over stone. I place a kiss on the smooth skin above his trousers. No bellybutton. I scoot backwards and cradle his foot in my lap. My fingers tug at the laces below his knee.

This time, his clothes are coming off first.

"Wait," he says, slowly, as if stirring from a stupor. "Knives."

He plucks three from one boot, two from the other—one my carving knife so when the hell did he get that?—and two more appear magically from somewhere in his trousers.

Maybe he's magnetic.

I tease his boot off and massage my thumb into the delicate arch of his sole. His eyes widen. I knead firm circles from heel to toes. Hunter melts in the chair, his wings black liquid in the candlelight.

Has he had no tenderness at all, not even a foot rub?

I massage him until he's at risk of sliding out of the seat. Then I de-boot his other foot and do the same. His eyes are closed, his breathing deep. I run my hands up his long, long legs to his waist. His eyelids flutter. I un-knot the laces at his crotch. His eyes snap open, tension singing in previously loose muscles. I hook my fingers under his waistband and peel the trousers from him, with some assistance.

Then I just look.

He's an angel carved of darkness and marble. My gaze drops

and a blush heats my cheeks.

Sweet lord. He's not going to fit.

I place my hands on his thighs, and he jumps. His fingers clench on the arm rests. Similar to before I removed his bandages. Then, he was ready to catapult himself from the chair. Today, I suspect he's fighting not to thrust his groin in my face.

Has he ever had oral? Giving, even willingly, is a form of losing in his culture. And if he never gets to demand...

Now I know why my first boyfriend got overexcited about my virginity. The power is exhilarating.

Hunter deserves a spectacular blowjob. Not that I like to brag. Then he can nap for a few hours and we can move on to the really fun stuff. After I limber up.

I bend my head close enough to breathe on him. He's so rigid, he's vibrating.

"Are you sure you want—"

I kiss taut, silky skin and say, "I want."

"Oh, Creators," he sighs.

"Hey, don't beseech those rapey bastards."

"Then who?"

"Who do you think?" I keep eye contact and lick the head of him.

"Maia," he says in a strangled voice that tingles in my chest and squirms through my belly.

Man, it's tempting to tease him. But teasing may be too excruciating for someone starved of affection.

I take a deep breath, pray I don't dislocate my jaw, and suck him into my mouth.

22

The noise Hunter makes has me squirming against the cage of his legs, pleasure pulsing deep in my belly. Plastic cracks. The arm rests fracture under the pressure of his fingers.

Think I'll just ignore that.

My heart flutters into my mouth but has nowhere to go. The tip of Hunter bumps the back of my throat and I wrestle my gag reflex into submission.

Jesus. I'm not even close to claiming him all. Deep-throating would take him half-way to my bellybutton and I doubt I have the skills.

I slide up for a gulp of air, swirling my tongue across him, and force myself a little deeper on each down-stroke. My hand curls around his shaft so the rest of him doesn't get lonely since, let's be honest, it's not going to happen with my mouth.

Less Hunter the human hunter, more Hunter the impaler.

I peek at him while I bob my head and tell myself I look majestic, not ridiculous.

His eyes excite and terrify me. Wild, hungry, *black*, the pupil devouring the midnight-blue. Something predatory stares at me. Something that sees no difference between tearing flesh, and fucking. Both would sate it. I may not survive either.

But I know what I'd prefer.

I cup Hunter's balls in my hand and tug, harder than I usually would. A sound rumbles in his chest, half-growl, half-groan. In one blink, firm hands grip my upper arms and propel me backwards. Wings flap. My arse hits the air mattress and a very naked, very aroused angel lands on top of me. Hands trap my wrists above my head, arching my body beneath him. He buries his face in my neck and all I can see over his shoulder are his wings.

"I do not think—I can be gentle," he pants.

Goosebumps prickle, warring with a wave of heat. My pulse thuds against his lips and leaps at the scrape of teeth. I swallow four times before I can speak.

"One thing to remember," I squeak, and do a little wiggle. "Fragile human." My fingers tap his hands where they pin my wrists. "Warrior angel."

A shudder runs through him, whispering in his feathers. Anxiety hollows my stomach but the heady throb of desire dampens the fear.

Maybe sex *is* a battle. I just need to make sure we both win.

Hunter sits up slowly, releasing my wrists and straddling my waist. The predator stalks behind his eyes but Hunter is there. The Hunter who hasn't hurt me since I helped him. Candlelight gilds the curve of muscle and surrenders to shadow in the hollows. He grips my hoodie zipper and draws it down. Strong fingers spread the sides open and tug it out from under me. I wince at his light stroke below my ribs.

"Fragile," he says.

A maroon bruise paints my skin where the pommel punched into me. It's going to be a lovely purple tomorrow.

Hunter traces the mark with a finger and more goosebumps flare. He chases them across my ribs and over my bra, my nipples stiff beneath the material. His hands skim to my waist and he removes my jeans, taking my underwear with them.

When did I last shave? I hope he likes stubble.

He kneels between my thighs, inching them apart with his legs. My shaky fingers unhook my bra and toss it aside.

No going back now.

"You are so tiny," he whispers. "Where will it go?"

"I admit, I have some concerns."

He flashes me a grin and I'm glad I'm lying down. The humour darkens to a hunger so intense, my settling pulse scurries in a panic. Hunter pins me with his gaze and dips his thumb between my legs, sliding upwards to circle that wonderful bud of nerves. The blanket bunches in my fists, my eyes fluttering shut. A finger slides inside me. Two. Holy crap—three. His thumb strokes my clitoris to the rhythm of his fingers. I buck against his hand, warmth spreading, swelling, throbbing—

Oh, *yes,* it's been so long.

I quiver on the edge of orgasm, my spine bowed, cheek pressed to the pillows, eyes shut tight.

The hand disappears.

A whine bursts out. "Hun-*ter.*"

I will kick his arse, warrior angel or no warrior angel.

Hunter smirks when I finally manage to open my eyes. He braces his hands on either side of me, too tall for face-to-face missionary. The tip of him eases between my legs. I bite my lip. He fights my body—hell, *his* body. His arms shake, sweat slicks his skin, but he slides deeper. Slow. Slow and careful. It's excruciating. So tight, so full. I've never felt anything like it.

"Oh, fuck," I moan.

He freezes, something close to panic on his face. He starts to pull away and I wrap my legs around his waist.

"Don't you dare stop," I say.

He shudders and it sends me writhing, my muscles clenching around him, which sends me writhing...

"Not hurting?" he says, his voice more strained than when I had his dick in my mouth.

"Not hurting," I say.

My breath wobbles out, shaken by my heartbeat. I tilt my hips and take Hunter in as far as he'll go. His eyes widen.

He needs no further encouragement.

There's a lot of him to glide in and out of me. He finds a rhythm, both glorious and punishing. His wings flick on each thrust and that extra flex of muscle drives him deeper, rubs him over some magical spot inside me. Air from his wings strokes my fevered skin and the sensation is almost too much. Pleasure builds, aches. I grunt at each slap of our bodies, like an idiot, though it seems to give him some trouble.

I can't keep quiet. It feels too good.

The normally implacable Hunter trembles above me, his control stripped by raw need. His expression is as naked as the rest of him.

Oh, Christ, I'm whimpering now.

My hands grip his arms, caress lean muscle. Effort quivers beneath my palms. He's still holding back. He has to. I'm not strong enough to survive him otherwise.

Part of me mourns that he can never truly lose himself, not with me.

I drive myself harder, faster, dancing on the line between pleasure and pain and it spills me over the edge. I scream his name in our tiny room, my nails raking his skin. Pleasure blinds me, heat blasting outward to leave me limp. Hunter collapses and I pant into his collarbone, his heart thundering against my cheek. Aftershocks ripple to torture my poor body.

I'm going to be sore tomorrow but give myself a mental high five. Worth it.

Hunter flops onto his back and I blink at the ceiling, sweat cooling in the sudden chill. He wasn't kidding when he said angels don't hug, not even after sex.

Well, I'm no angel.

I roll across his wing and cuddle into his side. He hesitates but his arms come around me. I snuggle closer, consciousness already slipping away, my body heavy, sated. A fading throb. Hunter's wings curl around us, softer, warmer than any blanket. His lips brush the top of my head.

"Thank you," he whispers, and I drop into sleep.

23

I wake in darkness with a heart thudding under my ear. I've climbed completely on top of Hunter in my sleep. I bob up and down with his ribs as he breathes. His hands rest on my back, one on my shoulder blade and one on the curve of my arse. He smells like a winter's day but his skin is summer heat.

Is he awake?

"I worried you were comatose," he says, and I jump.

A dull ache flares in low places. Not unpleasant. More like after a good workout. All I need are some stretches, maybe a massage...

"How long—day—time—what?"

Wow. I've been banged into incoherence.

"Try again, Maia," Hunter says.

I can hear the smirk in his voice. It seems the male satisfaction of a job well done is the same across all species.

I shove up on one arm and scrape a tickle of hair off my face. In the unrelieved blackness, I can't tell if my eyes are open. No light creeps around the door or where I imagine the door to be.

"How long did I sleep?"

"It is late morning."

There's something erotic about his voice in the dark. Rich

velvet thick enough to tease my skin. I shiver and his hands tighten. Excitement clenches my stomach, my muscles a little sore.

"How can you tell?" I say, my voice breathier than usual but not quite a squeak.

Not yet.

I should probably rest more. Bathe. Take paracetamol.

"I can feel the sun."

"You *feel* the sun?"

"And the moon."

My mouth flaps. I herd it closed.

"What's it like?"

Half of his chest jerks. A shrug?

"The sun pushes; the moon pulls. They chase each other across the sky."

"That's almost poetic."

"What is poetic?"

My turn to smirk. "I really need to expand your vocabulary. Teach you to read."

"You would teach me?" he says softly.

"If you want me to."

Silence stretches, made longer by the blackness, the lack of visual clues. Not that his face ever gives me much.

Except during sex.

"I want," he says, half-growl, half-purr.

My body pulses in response and my breath wobbles out. I reach for Hunter. My fingers find the smooth plane of a cheek and trace it to his lips. He lies still, solid, beneath me. I swap my fingers for my mouth, bumping his nose since I'm blind.

His lips seem softer, every touch magnified in the darkness. My fingers twine through silken hair, circle the delicate shell

142

of an ear. His jaw lacks the rasp of stubble, muscles working as he kisses me back and pleasure does a slow roll through my belly. I sit up, hands splayed on his chest, my very naked self pressed to his flat stomach.

"I want to finish what I started yesterday," I say, bold in the black.

"We did finish."

A grin stretches my mouth. "We did. But this time you're going to finish somewhere else."

I imagine him cocking his head while he puzzles that out. I turn carefully on top of him to face his feet and shuffle backwards, brushing the edge of his sprawled wings. His hands tickle my calves and dip into the sensitive spot behind my knees, the touch sending tingles between my legs. I drop to my elbows, my fingers on his hips, and the tension in his body says he has some clue what I'm doing. The position sticks my arse in the air and I'm glad he can't see—

Dammit. He's getting an eyeful of all sorts of intimate areas. Don't think about it.

I lower my head. If it were anyone else, there's a risk I'd miss but there's a lot of Hunter to find, even hampered by the dark. My lips nuzzle the hard length of him. His breath catches, loud in the stillness. I wriggle further and suck him into my mouth, both hands curled around him. He tastes of ice and salt.

How much is me and how much is him?

I ease into a rhythm, squeezing with my hands, sucking, licking, all the way up and all the way—okay, part of the way—down. His hips buck under my arms but the stop of my hands prevents unwanted choking.

Fingers grip my waist and hoist me aloft. I yelp around him, slapping a hand down to keep from impaling myself.

He pulls me backwards, my body stretched above him, the position quivering in my stomach muscles, already tight from yesterday's exertions. His mouth finds me, the contact heightened in the darkness.

So this is a sixty-nine. What do I taste like? Our sex from last night. The stress of battle. Unsated arousal from the cupboard. I'm not exactly at my freshest.

The lap of his tongue says Hunter doesn't mind. I give a long, *long* moan, my mouth and hand still wrapped around him. He draws me closer, the ache of my muscles sensitising every caress, pleasure swelling from the press of his lips. I can't stop squirming. Can't stop moaning. Frantic desire shivers between us while he drinks me down and I suck hard. He groans against me and his loss of control is so sexy, so vulnerable, it catapults me over the edge. My scream is muffled by my mouthful of Hunter, my body convulsing in his hands. I'm vaguely aware of him spurting deep in my throat then things are hazy for a while.

I may actually be comatose.

I come to sprawled on top of him, my cheek pillowed on his thigh, feathers tickling my shins and feet. Everything tingles, my muscles liquid. Hunter's breathing slows while I try to decide if I can move and conclude that, nope, I'm here for the day.

Hunter sits up, juggling my floppy limbs in his hands until he cradles me in his lap, my spine against his chest, both of us slippery.

"I like the noises you make," he says.

He palms my breasts and I reward him with a whimper. He drapes my legs over his and spreads them wide. Something very long and very hard slides in the crack of my arse.

23

"Again?" I squeak. "Don't you need to rest?"

Lips curve against my temple. "I do not need to rest."

Lord have mercy.

Softness brushes my legs, tickling up my thighs. Velvet caresses my apex and I gasp.

"You'll get your feathers all sticky."

"I like sticky."

His fingers tilt my chin and his mouth claims mine, my spine arching to reach him. He shifts me in his lap and the head of him teases my opening, drawing another gasp but he is merciless, swallowing the sound and slipping inside me. I'm wet from his mouth, wet from me. One hand pins me against him, the other sliding between my legs.

And so starts the moaning.

In this position, the angle is shallower, his power limited. Only the flick of his wings and the roll of his hips rock us together, each thrust rubbing me against his hand. He kisses me with tongue, lips, teeth. I struggle to breathe, mostly because any air is immediately used for whimpering. My heart shudders through my entire body, my skin buzzes. Everything throbs outward from where he's gliding inside me.

It's too much. I can't take it.

Oh, *Christ,* I don't want him to stop even though I'm dizzy, breathless. Aching.

When did I last eat or drink? I may pass out this time.

His rhythm falters. His hand massages me in desperate circles. He growls low in his throat and it vibrates into me. His hips thrust harder. The wind from his wings strokes swollen skin. I freeze on the precipice and the next swirl of his fingers, his tongue, the slide of him inside me, shoves me over. I toss my head, ripping my mouth from his, and scream his name to the dark. He falls with me and my name is almost a sob.

24

"Where does your culture stand on masturbation?" I say.

"What is—"

"You know, touching yourself until you orgasm?"

Hunter cocks his head, sprawled in the chair, the candles burning low and casting shadows in his cheekbones. I lie on the air mattress, naked, a blanket pulled to my chin.

"It is more shameful than refusing a challenge," he says.

"But what if you don't get to orgasm? You could go months without climax. Years."

He raises a brow. "Do not lose."

"Let me guess—the sicker bastards made it part of the torture. The She-devil, for example."

He gives me a grim smile. "She excelled at it. They would beg. Do anything."

"Did you?"

"I did not beg."

"How long?" I say. "How long did that bitch keep you from release?"

His gaze drops. He picks an imaginary piece of fluff from his trousers.

"Ten of your years," he says without looking at me.

"And that ended with me?"

Black eyes meet mine and my heart skips.

"It was obvious?" he says.

"Not in the slightest. I'm amazed at your restraint."

His smile is almost shy. "You are fragile human."

"Well, let's break more bad habits from your toxic society."

I toss the blanket off. Cool air tightens my skin and hardens two little buds in particular. Hunter shifts from sprawled relaxation to predatory alertness in one nanosecond. His hands clench on the already destroyed arm rests.

I wag my finger at him. "You stay right there."

"Why?" he growls.

The hunger in his eyes thrills me. All he has to do is look at me like he wants to eat me and I puddle on the floor. Different to our first night where I was afraid he would, literally, eat me. His appetite may push me to my limits and have my body weeping for mercy but he never hurts me.

I stretch, my eyes half-lidded and on Hunter, my muscles limber, a pleasant ache in my stomach and between my legs. Evidence of his skills.

"Do you want to fuck me, Hunter?"

"Yes," he says.

I love that he doesn't lie or pussy-foot around. He may evade but he deserves some secrets.

He thrusts forward in the seat, elbows on his knees, his arse perched on the edge. His wings flare wide.

"You can only watch," I say, my voice husky. "You can't touch until…"

I swear, he's close to launching himself off the chair. The heat of his gaze is enough to scald.

"Until what?" he says.

I lick my lips and he follows the movement.

"Until you make yourself come."

"Come where?"

I stifle a giggle. How can he be intense and cute at the same time?

"I mean you have to make yourself orgasm."

He shakes his head. I hope it's more dazed than disgusted.

"Masturbation isn't shameful, Hunter. I'll show you."

My own shame, so difficult to cleanse, raises its head but I squash it. Fundamentalist Catholics revel in sin and body-shaming. My father caught me exploring once and that experience was a million times worse than my first period. After his screaming sermon, he dragged me to church to confess and told his priest in front of a whole choir of boys practising for mass.

I was thirteen.

I fold the pillow and prop myself up. Hunter watches me like a great beast of prey, coiled to pounce. I arch my back and run my palms over my breasts and down my belly. My fingertips touch tight curls of hair. I bite my lip, my pulse jumping in the hollow of my throat.

Now *this* is the most erotic thing I've ever done.

"Touch yourself, Hunter," I whisper. "Then you get to touch me."

I slip my hand between my legs and the contact sizzles to my toes, the weight of Hunter's stare heightening my desire. He sways at my appreciative noise. I spread myself for him—legs, lips—so he can see exactly what my finger is doing.

Man, I'm wet.

He bows his head and his shoulders heave.

"My control is not infinite," he says through gritted teeth.

"Touch yourself. *Please.* I want to watch."

His hands drop to the laces at his waist. The anticipation throbs in my belly and I reward him with a moan, helped, somewhat, by my finger massaging my clitoris. Hunter leans back and loosens his trousers, shoving them down only far enough for his dick to spill out. His eyes lock on me. My finger glides on slick, soft flesh and I circle my opening, struggling to keep my eyelids from fluttering shut.

Hunter wraps his fist around his cock. He shudders and I pause to watch him, ridiculously close to coming myself just from the sight of it. He looks at his hand, all that hard, straining length, as if it doesn't belong to him. He gives himself an experimental stroke and his breath catches, his gaze flying to me.

"Hunter," I whimper, "you look so. Fucking. *Hot.*"

He manages a smirk, boneless in the chair, his hand working faster until he gives a little moan of his own.

"You may have to hurry," I gasp, "or I'm going to finish way before you. Whoever comes first, wins."

The slap of his hand increases. Taut muscles gleam in his stomach and chest, the cords of his neck tense.

"What will I win?" he grinds out.

"Whatever you want."

"What do you want?"

"You. Inside me. But until then, this will do."

I slide my finger deep. Hunter makes a begging sound low in his throat but I'm writhing on the air mattress with my eyes shut. When I manage to focus on him, his hand is a blur, his hips pumping. I'm mesmerised by the bunch and release of his abs. His wings quiver and his head lolls on the seat, his eyes glittering half-moons of black.

He's winning. It turns me on so goddamn much.

I stroke that sensitive spot inside me, the heel of my hand rubbing my mound. A warm heaviness expands in my gut, tingling outward, clenching muscle and slicking skin.

"Maia," Hunter groans.

His powerful body spasms in the chair, and metal creaks. He beats me by a millisecond. Then I'm squirming and my attention slips to the explosive rush, leaving me limp and trembling. Our panting slows in the cosy, candlelit room. I roll my head to look at Hunter. He grins and dives for me. I yelp. Can't help it. Sixty kilos of half-naked angel pins me to the air mattress.

"I win," he says, nuzzling my mouth. "And I am all sticky."

25

"Why do your creators think it's their business to police the universes? Why do they care?"

I'm lying on my back, my head pillowed on Hunter's shoulder, his arms cuddling me against the rest of him. Soft candlelight flickers on the walls of the security room. The tips of Hunter's wings twitch lazily.

"They were the first intelligent life," he says.

"And that gives them the right to judge the rest?"

Hunter shakes his head. "They are neutralising potential threats before they can pollute the other universes. They created the Protectorate to protect. It is our duty."

The redhead that stabbed the Pope in the eye and murdered the baby said the same—protection and duty. Our day of reckoning for not reversing the damage. I can't deny we've abused our planet—our universe—but did they have to be so smug about punishing us? Wiping out billions of people hardly seems to fit the crime.

"Do you still believe that?" I say softly.

He tilts his chin to look at me. From this angle, he's all dark eyes and cheekbones.

"Maybe there are other ways to protect," he says.

I said something similar when I rescued him from the

shackles, when he asked me why I was helping him—we need to find a solution that doesn't involve killing each other.

Though I would like to teach the damn Creators a lesson for choosing war over peace.

"I doubt the other angels are interested in becoming pacifists," I say.

Hunter's chest rumbles under my head, almost a chuckle. "No. They live for the battle."

"How close are they to their target?"

"Not as close as they would like."

I sigh. "So it could be months before they leave."

Hunter strokes my arms but says nothing. My skin tingles under the sweep of his fingers.

"And the longer they stay, the more likely it is for them to find us," I continue. "Persipha knows about this place. What if she comes back? How am I supposed to protect you from her?"

Hunter's tickling caress stills on my arms. "You want to protect me?"

Jeez, how ridiculous does that sound? Me, the tiny, fragile human offering to protect the semi-invincible warrior angel. How insulting.

I clear my throat. "I don't want them to hurt you anymore."

Hunter shifts underneath me. I bob on the air mattress as he props himself up, my head nestling in the crook of his elbow. He looms over me, formed of blackness and wings.

"You would protect me?" he says.

I try to get a hint of what he's feeling from his tone, his expression, but both are impassive.

"I mean, I'm not much of a shield or skilled in hand-to-hand combat but if there was a way to get rid of them, I would. Same for your creators—I don't want you anywhere near them ever again."

"We have never been defeated." Hunter frowns at a spot on the air mattress beyond my left shoulder.

"Of course you haven't."

"No, Maia." He raises his gaze. "That is how to get rid of us."

I huff out a breath. "How are we supposed to defeat you? I thought the weakness to iron would be enough but the last I saw, hardly any angels were dying."

"You do not need to kill all of us," he says. "Kill enough of us and our creators will panic."

I shove up onto my hands and nearly headbutt him in the jaw. His arms come around to steady me, his wings a comforting shadow. I stare into his face from inches away.

"What are you saying?"

His mouth quirks. "We are too difficult to replace."

"How many are we talking—ten, a hundred?"

He shrugs. "I do not think it would take much, not if it happened all at once."

And just like that, hide and seek becomes a race. Who will reach their target first?

"Why are you telling me this?" I whisper.

Hunter's fingers slide through my hair. He dips his head.

"This is how I protect you," he says.

His lips slant across mine. I melt into the kiss and right into his lap. I peel myself away before I get distracted by firm muscle and hot skin.

"But we've been trying to kill you this whole time," I say, breathless already. "People die from arrows before they can get close enough."

Hunter smirks. "You did not have me before."

"And I have you now?"

The smirk widens, heat sparking in his eyes. He grips my hips and presses me harder into his lap. My pulse shatters into a thousand, throbbing pieces.

"You have me," he says.

26

"You look different." Steph hands me a cup of tea, the water freshly boiled on her camping stove.

I feel different. Powerful. A ten-foot-tall Amazonian instead of a petite woman who can wear kids' shoes. I already have more muscle definition from all the, ahem, exercise.

I glance at Hunter. He's sitting in Steph's black, massage chair, cradling a mug in his hands. A single candle flickers on the coffee table, the curtains shut against the night. Steph follows my gaze.

She greeted us at the door. A warm hug for me and a cool nod for Hunter.

"So, you sampled the merchandise," she says, her brow raised.

My cheeks flame and I bury my face in my cup, pretending it's the steam. Hunter blinks before his implacable expression slips into place.

"I did not hurt," he says.

He's proud of himself and I want to hug him. It's such a huge step coming from a culture of pain and dominance. *I'm* proud of him.

"No, she's not hurt," Steph says, somewhat reluctantly. "Maia, hell, you look like that's all you've been doing this past week."

I clear my throat. "Um…"

He managed to play with me on the flight over, too, his hands under my clothes. The chance of falling, the rush of danger, his skilled fingers, all combined into the most intense orgasm.

He gives because he can, not because he has to. And I'll reciprocate. He's learned that now and knows I won't snatch it from him at the last minute, unlike some colossal bitch I could mention.

Steph lowers herself onto the couch beside me, slipping her cane into the special holster we made on that wine-soaked, bedazzling afternoon. She's wearing a blood-red, zip-front velour tracksuit that goes great with her chestnut wig.

That confused Hunter when she opened the door. She had pale hair when we met, though he could probably tell the exact colour with his super-duper night vision.

She blows on her tea and takes a sip. "I admit, I'm a little jealous."

Hunter's eyes widen. I drink my tea to drown a giggle.

"What's he like?" she says.

"Steph, he's sitting right there."

"We could go in my bedroom. The apocalypse doesn't seem to be ruining your sex life. I need details."

Panic flits across Hunter's face.

I snort into my cup. "Don't be mean to him."

"He's different, too. What have you done?" Her gaze sweeps him from head to toe. "Besides the obvious."

He's wearing his usual boots and trousers, cleaned a few times since we kept getting them sticky. He has a grey hoodie on with nothing underneath and slits up the back for his wings. He grumbled that it wasn't black but it suits him.

I shrug one shoulder. "I was nice to him."

"I said besides the obvious."

Another blush. Another gulp of tea.

"So we're past the chest-poking stage?"

"For now." She smiles sweetly at Hunter. "He could be a spy."

"I'm hardly the leader of the resistance."

"Aren't you?"

My mug pauses half-way to my mouth. "That's actually what we wanted to talk to you about."

"We?"

"Yes, *we*. He's on our side. There's no love lost between him and his people."

"How sure are you of that? He could—"

"What is love?"

Hunter's quiet voice silences our bickering. I open and close my mouth.

"Yes, Maia," Steph smirks, "why don't you explain love to the alien creature?"

Honestly, if there were such an award, she and Hunter would be in close competition for Smirker of the Year.

I shoot her a glare. "It's, um, a feeling... When two people care for each other..."

"I'll get the dictionary," she says.

I wrap my fingers around her arm before she can stand. She grins at me and I roll my eyes. Hunter's gaze flicks between us.

"It's an intense emotional attachment," I say, and will myself not to blush. "Tenderness, affection, concern for another person. Or, um, creature."

"Nice save," Steph whispers out the corner of her mouth.

"Basically, when you love someone, you can't imagine your life without them. It's a feeling, right here." I touch my hand to my heart. "You'd do anything for them."

I can't meet Hunter's gaze. My pulse misbehaves when I do

158

and this is not the time to dissect my response.

"*Any*-way," I say, drawing the word out, "back to the resistance. Have you had much activity, angel-wise, since we were here?"

Steph shakes her head. "It's been quiet. Maybe they've left."

I look at Hunter. He sits with his elbows on his knees, staring into his mug, his wings arching over his shoulders. He glances up.

What is he thinking? And why does it make me nervous?

"They have not left," he says. "They are not finished."

"We need to get people together," I say. "Form organised groups. Turn the angels from hunters to hunted. If enough of them die, Hunter thinks his creators will abort the mission. They're too expensive and time-consuming to replace."

Steph eyes all of Hunter perched in her chair.

"No shit," she says.

"Can you gather everyone from the flats tomorrow? Meet in the parking garage?"

Steph nods. "It's more than just us in Martello Court. We've been trying to contact survivors, pass on our details, but it's a slow, sporadic process dialling numbers on sat phones."

"Then it's time we all got coordinated."

We finish our tea. The clock in the kitchen ticks the silent minutes. Hunter's focus fixes on me. I struggle to think of an excuse to stay longer. He's going to ask questions I'm not ready to answer.

Steph yawns and gathers the empty cups.

Crap.

"Do you need anything while we're here?" I say a little too quickly. "Want us to bring you anything?"

"You've brought enough. Those painkillers are working

nicely and I'm not going to run out of food, though I may get sick of pasta and noodles. I miss apples. Tinned fruit is shit."

I grin at her. "Amen. I'm craving mangoes like you wouldn't believe."

Before I know it, we're heading for the door, Hunter at the rear since he hates people at his back.

People he doesn't trust yet, anyway.

I check the hallway through the peephole and open the door. Hunter sidles past Steph, adjusting his sword to avoid scraping the wall.

"Hunter," she says, and he stops. She leans on her cane and holds out a hand. "Thank you—for keeping her safe. Sorry for all the poking."

He cocks his head. I guide his hand to hers and show him how to shake. She definitely shivers when his palm touches hers.

"You are best friends," he says. "I understand the poking."

"And you." She pulls me into a hug to whisper the last in my ear. "Tell him the truth, if he asks."

"I don't know what you're talking about."

"We're best friends," she says as if that explains everything.

And maybe it does.

27

Hunter stays quiet during the flight back and during the walk to the security room and once the door clicks shut. He sits on the—much abused—swivel chair and watches me getting ready for bed, which mostly involves taking clothes off rather than putting them on like in the old days post-electric heater and pre-Hunter.

He likes to cuddle. I wake, cocooned in the curve of his body, his arms and wings wrapped around me. He keeps me warm and safe. He also enjoys morning sex in that position. He can let his hands wander.

I peek at him through my lashes. The urge to say something bubbles in my throat. It's impossible to be silent under the intensity of his gaze.

No. I won't talk. If he has something on his mind, he can spill it.

"What're you thinking?" I say.

Well, crap.

His eyes are unflinching, his face unreadable.

I've learned it means he's pondering something. His arrogant face is for when he's threatened, or confused, and he doesn't want the other person to know what he's feeling.

"Do you love?" he says.

My heart flaps against my ribs.

Dammit. I should've kept my mouth shut.

"I've only had two relationships," I babble. "I didn't love either of them."

Hunter shifts in the seat. I'm very aware of his hips, the line of his thighs. His wings stretch and brush the floor.

He uses them for foreplay, tickling across my skin. It's amazing.

"Come here," he says.

A thrill fizzes to my toes.

My whole life, I was told how to think, how to behave, how certain, completely-freaking-normal actions were shameful. But Hunter ordering me about? Glorious. Especially as it always leads to him doing wonderful things to me. Turns out I enjoy being dominated. And he's great at it.

Other angels really are stupid.

He nudges my legs apart and pulls me into his lap until I straddle him. I stroke his chest, sliding his zipper down without conscious thought, my fingers petting solid muscle under warm skin. He smirks and his hands fall to my hips, pressing me close.

"Do you love now?" he says.

"Sex isn't the same as love," I squeak, "though it's part of it."

His hands glide under my t-shirt and up my back. His lips find mine, the kiss as intense as the rest of him.

Another thing he's great at.

"Do you love?" he whispers against my mouth.

I lick my lips and him in the process. "Do you?"

"I am built for war."

Oh man, I'm an idiot. A naive, bleeding-hearted romantic. Steph got that right. Hunter was made to be a weapon, not a man. Or a boyfriend.

Jesus Christ.

I duck my head and hide my face in his neck. His pulse beats against my hot cheek.

"But I love," he says.

I jerk upright. "You what?"

"I love"—he cocks his head—"you."

My mouth drops open. He can't be serious. He found out what it meant an hour ago. He must think it's true because he's fond of me. The only one who was nice to him.

And I'm sure the blowjobs help.

"I love that you are fragile and I could break you," he says.

"Um…"

"I love that I have to be careful. That I can be gentle."

"Hunter, that's just sexual intimacy. Granted, it can be confused—"

His fingers knead my shoulder blades and I melt into his lap. He seems to be *very* happy with how the conversation is going.

"I love that I can do anything and you do not view me as weak."

"Maybe not anything…"

He gives me a tiny shake, his hands cupping my ribs, his thumbs grazing my bra.

"I love," he says. "I *love*."

And he grins. A proper, full-blown, uninhibited grin. It softens the harsh planes of his face and sparkles a million stars in his eyes.

I reach for him in a daze and kiss his smiling mouth—teeth and lips and all. His arms curl around me then his wings and I'm wrapped in a cocoon of Hunter. I struggle to breathe, partly due to his strength but mostly because I'm snogging him like there's no tomorrow.

And maybe there isn't. This *is* the apocalypse.

Hunter buries his face in my hair.

"You make me fit in," he says in my ear.

"Well," I gasp, "it's still a bit of a squeeze, to be honest."

He's completely still for two heartbeats. A sound rumbles in his chest. It vibrates upwards and a chuckle spills from his mouth to warm my scalp.

"I do not mean sex, Maia."

He nibbles my lobe and I squirm in his lap. He draws away enough to look at me.

"There is nowhere I fit in but here. With you."

Then he's kissing me and I'm fumbling at the laces of his trousers. I jump off his lap to shuck my clothes and straddle him, naked, before he can do more than shimmy his trousers past his hips.

And, just like he said, he fits.

His eyes widen, his fingers gripping my waist as he slides deep. I lose myself in him. The noises he makes—his are much better than mine—his intoxicating scent. The way he holds me, delicate even when his control slips. My name a prayer on his lips. We break our fastest record by about five minutes. Afterwards, I find myself cradled by his body, with no memory of how we got to be on the air mattress. His heart slows against my spine.

"Do you love?" he says.

I smile and wriggle closer, hugging his arms.

"I love," I say.

28

"I'm not sure about this."

My voice echoes in the parking garage. Dim light filters from the ramp entrance, guarded by Greg and his stoner friend, Mikey. Steph stops shaking her spray canister and cocks an eyebrow at me. She has her rainbow wig—my personal favourite—in a tight ponytail, a few strands falling to the strong line of her jaw and framing her face.

"It's just chalk, Maia. He says he's fine with it. You're fine with it, right?" She directs her cocked eyebrow at Hunter.

He spreads his wings. "It is camouflage—like you humans use in war."

"But what if it affects your flight? What if you get over-whelmed and can't fly away?"

"I will fight my way out."

"See—he's fine with it," Steph says, and they share a smirk.

I sigh. "I'm not sure I like this pally version of you two. Seems I'll get ganged up on."

"It's sweet that you worry about your indestructible angel boyfriend."

"Semi-indestructible," I huff, shaking my paint can.

I slip my mask over my nose and Steph does the same. Hunter's mask dangles from his fingers.

I nod at him. "Put it on. You don't want to inhale this stuff."

"What's he going to get, lung cancer?" Steph snorts.

"I've stumbled on one thing that hurts him already. I don't want to discover another when his insides dissolve."

Hunter flashes a smile but indulges me.

"Okay, now for the skin test," I say.

Steph's eyes crinkle above her mask. "Wow. You really are soft for him, aren't you?"

I slide her a glare, though it doesn't keep my cheeks from flushing. White chalk hisses from the can and coats a couple of feathers at the tip of Hunter's wing.

"If it stings or feels weird, dip it in the water." I kick the bucket, making the surface dance.

Hunter's wing sweeps me into the heat of his body and his arms curl around me. I snuggle into the warmth and ice, and listen to his heartbeat.

He's wearing a blue shirt. A massive concession to match the rest of his disguise. He refused to change the rest.

I can get him out of his trousers for sex but not for this, apparently. Why do I find that cute?

"It does not feel weird," he says.

I catch Greg giving me the side-eye, his rusty chain swinging beside his leg.

You'd think he'd be used to it by now.

The last two weeks have been a blur of preparation. My first meeting with the rest of Martello Courts' residents—and the other, widespread groups Steph's communication network managed to contact—was mostly their conniption at Hunter and their grumbling after I told them to get over it. We spread outward, gathering other survivors, sending feelers further and further into the quieter, post-angel world.

It was time to stop hiding.

We used the generators found by Steph's group to keep the radios and sat phones charged and spoke to anyone we could find on the other end. I organised the different groups into shifts to methodically work through the lists of numbers. My best connection was a man in Nova Scotia. He didn't know about iron. I asked him to spread the word, gather weapons and, like everyone else we spoke to, fight on the 25th of December. Today.

Merry Christmas.

"If you two could quit canoodling," Steph says, "we have a tight schedule."

I ease out of Hunter's arms. "Yes, Boss."

"I'm not the boss," she says, and I don't need to see her mouth to know she's smirking. "I'm the glamorous assistant."

Hunter stretches his wings. Our canisters rattle in the silence. I depress the nozzle and spray his feathers. The hiss fills the cavernous space. Three cans sputter empty to cover each wing and I toss my last one on the concrete. Chalk dust settles. Hunter flicks his wings and a cloud puffs around him.

The colour isn't perfect—grey in some places, black streaks—but it should be enough to fool the others.

Hunter tugs off his mask to examine his feathers.

"I always wanted to look like them," he says, and his gaze meets mine. "But I suspect they would have hated me, no matter the colour."

He's certainly more angelic, despite the black hair and dark eyes. The ethereal whiteness glows against his skin.

"Do you think you can fly?"

He takes a couple of experimental flaps, buffeting me with wind. His toes leave the concrete. Dust swirls in mini-tornadoes and I remind myself it's chalk, not the remains of people.

His boots hit the floor. "Flying will not be a problem."

Steph and I remove our masks. She limps a couple of steps and sinks into her wheelchair. Her dagger hangs from the armrest in a sheath.

"We're ready, Greg," she says.

Greg lopes down the ramp, his chain clanking over his shoulder. A twinkling gold length of tinsel holds his long hair in a loose ponytail in honour of the day. He wraps his fingers around the handles of Steph's chair.

I bend and pull her into a quick hug. "Be careful. Stay out of sight. Don't show yourself unless you're sure they're out of arrows."

"You're the one who needs to be careful," she huffs in my ear.

"Don't worry. I have an angel watching over me."

I straighten and we both look at Hunter, his face intense and arrogant now that Greg has joined us.

"Are you sure he's the only nice one?" Steph says. "It hardly seems fair."

I grin at her. "Maybe see if they try to kill you before you ask if they want a girlfriend."

"Or stick to humans," Greg says, his lip curled.

"You offering?"

A flush rises in his face. "N-no. You ain't my type."

"Not woman enough?"

"Too much woman," he mutters, and heaves her chair up the ramp.

She waves like a departing queen and disappears into the grey, wintry day with Greg and Mikey. Heat brushes my shoulders and I lean into Hunter.

"Do you think this'll work?"

He rests his chin on the top of my head. "It may not be today but kill enough and they should go."

"How will we know?"

"I will hear it."

I turn in his arms and ease back to look up at him. "Is this the same magical power that lets you feel the sun and the moon?"

"Not magical." He taps his temple. "Technological."

Oh, good. My boyfriend is a semi-indestructible warrior angel and also part cyborg. Way to feel inadequate.

"Is that how you learned about us so fast—they just downloaded the information directly into your brain?"

Hunter takes a couple of seconds to puzzle through the unfamiliar word then says, "Yes."

"Have they said anything since you got here?"

"No."

"Can you broadcast and tell them to bugger off?"

A smile tugs at his mouth. "No."

"That's disappointing. You're built for war but I'm not. I can't wait until this is over."

He bends his tall body and kisses me. "Perhaps you need some motivation."

He picks me up and I squeal before I can stop myself. The noise echoes and mocks me. I wrap my legs around his waist.

For balance.

"When this is over," he says, nibbling at my mouth, "I will need your help to remove my camouflage."

His wings whisper on my jacket.

I gulp. "You mean I get to bathe you?"

A wet Hunter. Oh, wow. Water beaded on his feathers, his hair, his eyelashes. His shirt moulded to his chest and abs before I peel it off. Warm, slippery skin...

I kiss his smirking mouth until I'm breathless.

"What the hell are we waiting for?" I gasp. "Let's go kick some angel arse."

29

My confidence fizzles as soon as I'm alone in the car. Which is a bummer. My Mitsubishi usually makes me feel unstoppable. Like I could go anywhere, road or no road.

I twist the key and the seat rumbles underneath me. The headlights blaze blue-white on Hunter's wings. The black string of a bow bisects his chest, the weapon stolen by a Martello Court resident from the bodies of the angels Hunter and I left behind a few weeks ago. The quiver holds ten iron-tipped arrows instead of soul-sucking swirly ones.

Somehow, our apocalypse has gone from a rout to an impasse and dragged on for a month and a half. Probably our fault for fighting back. If it goes on much longer, we'll have to start growing our own food.

I crack the window, the glass covered by wire mesh welded in place.

"Be careful," I whisper to my semi-indestructible warrior angel.

Hunter gives me a gentle smile.

"I have never had anyone worried for me before." He places his hand on the mesh and I match him. "I like it."

I fumble with my seatbelt and slip out of the car. Hunter's arms catch me, hold me tight, his mouth hot on mine.

"You are the fragile human," he says, "not me."

"You can still be hurt. You can still die."

"I will try not to." He trails a finger across my cheek and captures a tear. "You cry for me?"

"I love you."

He traces my lips and kisses me with the taste of salt between us.

"I love you, too," he says.

He waits until I'm back in the car then disappears out of the garage in a blur of white, black and blue. My breath wobbles.

It's business as usual for him—battle, violence, pain. I just want to be at Newhailes, snuggling him on the air mattress.

I take a steadier breath and motor up the ramp, peering through the wire mesh. Grey clouds greet me in a heavy, leaden sky. Snow ticks against the side of the car and sneaks through the mesh to streak the windscreen. I crane my neck and, of course, can't find Hunter.

But he's there.

I circle a roundabout of bare trees onto Pennywell Gardens, a strip of green separating the lanes of the road. Snow dusts the grass and settles on the concrete. I can't remember our last white Christmas. Hopefully, it's a good omen.

I turn right onto Pennywell Road, chuckling at myself for using the indicator. Who the hell else is here? The strip of green widens, lined by trees, their branches stippled brown and white.

Muirhouse and Pilton may seem like rough areas of Edinburgh but they're wide open, surprisingly green, and I've always loved the mix of people. Sure, some of them were arseholes but you get that everywhere. Today, those of us left fight together, arseholes and non-arseholes.

And one angel.

Ferry Road takes me past the police station where my band of warriors helped themselves to radios. I dodge a traffic snarl at Crewe Toll, weaving the wrong way around the roundabout. I shiver at the Western General passing on my right.

The guy will be dead. The one who begged I take him with me. A shrivelled skeleton in a lonely bed.

Well, no more. This is the start of the end.

I've barely entered Craigleith before my bright-red, moving car draws attention. The grey sky highlights a squadron of angels winging from the direction of the castle. Wind howls, splattering snow across the bonnet. I grab the radio in the cup holder and depress the button.

"I have contact. Steph, Greg—are you all in position?"

The radio crackles.

"Use our call signs," Greg says.

I drop the radio in my lap and execute a hasty three-point turn, bumping hard on the kerb. The space between my shoulder blades itches, though I can't see the angels through the closed bed of my pick-up.

I snatch the radio. "Valkyrie and Cheech, are you all in position?"

"Copy that, we are in position. But you need to identify yourself. So we know it's really you."

Greg sounds like he's enjoying himself but then he's hiding in a house surrounded by other people. He's not the bait.

Not yet.

"It's obvious it's me," I say. "You can hear my voice."

"Use your call sign."

"Greg—"

"*Cheech.*"

I sigh loudly into the receiver. "This is Angeltamer heading to your position. ETA ten minutes."

"There, that wasn't so hard."

"Shut up, Greg."

"Copy that, Angeltamer."

"Remember he wanted to call you something else," Steph says, a hint of laughter in her voice. "Just be thankful. Valkyrie, over and out."

I snort and drop the radio into the cup holder.

Greg's first suggestion was Angelfucker because I am, um, sleeping with one but also because we're about to go fuck the rest. His words. Mostly.

Steph slapped him upside the head and told him to shut it. We compromised on the name.

I steer my Mitsubishi into Muirhouse, slowing for the narrow roads and cars clogging the streets. Over the last few nights, we cleared the way of vehicles and created barricades of metal.

Flats steal the daylight to a slice of grey above me. Hedges border small gardens. I glimpse movement on the edge of a roof but don't dare look, my eyes fixed on the snow swirling on the tarmac.

"We see you, Angeltamer," Greg whispers. "Twelve bogeys gathering above you."

Bogeys? He's really getting into this assault stuff.

I focus on that instead of the number of angels surrounding me.

"Copy, Cheech. Switch to radio silence."

"Let's batter these fuckers," he hisses.

The road branches into a T-junction. An arrow thwacks into my windscreen, and I yelp. It bounces off the wire mesh, leaving a divot in the glass beneath. Another thuds somewhere. One cracks into the window near my face. I grit my teeth so hard, my jaw aches.

Four angels stand on the roof of a flat looking down at me, all sharp cheekbones and empty eyes. They aim their bows. Swirly blue roils into my stomach even though I can't hear the awful humming through the windows. The angel on the left topples. Then the next and the next. The last spins to look behind him and falls with an arrow in his eye. White and black flashes over the gap onto the roof opposite.

Hunter.

"Thirty more incoming," Mikey whispers, a wobble in his voice.

My throat clicks.

Sweet mother. We must have emptied the castle.

"Copy," I say. "Greg?"

"First enemy arrows destroyed. Tell your tame angel he can collect his."

I roll my eyes. Hunter is anything but tame.

The untamed beast in question dangles a white-winged angel off the edge of the roof, his hand around her throat, and stabs her in the chest with an iron arrow. Two stabs. Three, and the angel's wings droop. Hunter releases his grip on her neck and she thumps into a garden behind a hedge. I bleep my horn once. Hunter launches across the street to where the first bodies dropped to get his arrows back from whoever reclaimed them from the corpses.

We want to deplete their arrows, not ours.

Hunter vaults the hedge and thuds in the tiny gap between my Mitsubishi and a white Hyundai. He splays his hand on the mesh over the side window and I touch my palm to it, convinced I can feel the hot pulse of his skin through the chill of the glass. Silver blood and yellowish froth smear his face and speckle his off-white wings, none of it his. He smiles softly at me and leaps into the sky.

A volley of arrows darkens the clouds, arching towards Hunter. He spins and swoops out of sight, taking my heart with him. A group of ten follow.

"Start the runs," I squeak into the radio.

How in the hell did I become leader of the resistance?

A clanking increases through the windows. Another burst of wind buffets my stationary Mitsubishi, wailing down the gap between the buildings. My engine purrs. Warm air heats my toes.

Maybe I *am* the lucky one. At least I'm not in the cold.

Yet.

A stream of people weaves between the barricade of cars, shields hoisted above their heads—cabinet doors welded together, metal stripped from vehicles. A hodgepodge of other metal protects limbs and chests, clanking as they move. The people dash for the flats opposite, whoops spilling from their mouths in a ragged battle cry.

Arrows rain from above. My gloved fingers squeeze the steering wheel. The arrows twang into cars, thwap into shields or spin off. One slips through a gap between two frying pans. The guy trips, mouth wide and frozen, and crumbles with the snow. A woman falls, screaming, an arrow bristling from her shoulder. A man swerves and his hip bumps the corner of a van. His shield jerks from his hands. Arrows gouge his neck. He clutches at his throat and stumbles to his knees. Red stains the dust.

Hunter dives down the road, twisting his body to fire left and right. He blasts above my Mitsubishi in a swirl of snowflakes.

The survivors melt into the building to regroup. The next wave charges, sweeping around my car.

More arrows. More humans reduced to plant food. Each one is an ache in my chest.

Angels land in the road or on top of vehicles in a squeal of protesting metal. They draw swords of soul-sucking blue.

"Weapons ready," I bark into the radio, my fingers tightening on my sword.

The angels stalk towards the flats on both sides of the road, their skin carved of marble. Two creatures flank my Mitsubishi, one in front, the other at the side lunging for the rear door. I gun the engine. The angel in front jumps clear, swiping his sword down and cleaving paint from my bonnet.

Hunter stoops into the T-junction and tackles the angel, dragging him out of sight above me. A body slams onto the roof of a parked car. Golden feathers ruffle in the wind. Metal sings, the angel in my wing mirror straining to parry Hunter's sword. Hunter sweeps his blade clear and buries iron in the angel's skull.

More angels spill into the junction. Hunter spins through the air in a graceful arc and lands to block them, his laced boots skidding on the powdered snow. His blade whirls, parrying arrows that skitter away under vehicles. The angels charge, swords raised. Grim and arrogant and silent.

I mash my foot on the accelerator.

Figures scatter. A female falls. My tyres bump over her. A male sneers at me. Blue slices the fluttering snow. My Mitsubishi thuds into his body at the same time his sword flays metal in a flurry of sparks. I keep my foot pressed down and the engine roars, driving the angel on my bonnet backwards into the parked cars opposite the junction. The crunch shivers through my arse and my head jerks forward. The male struggles, pinned between the vehicles, his teeth bared. His sword hacks at my car. Cracks feather across the window.

I grab my shield and sword and leap into the cold. Screams and shouts echo from the buildings. Metal clashes everywhere. Hunter is lost behind the furious flapping of wings on the far side of the Mitsubishi. The pinioned angel spits at me. His sword flashes. Nausea tugs in my stomach. The evil blue blade clangs on my shield and I lunge underneath, skewering the angel's chest. Blood bursts and patters on the bonnet, melting the snow. The male sags. His sword clatters in the road.

The female growls, clawing at the sky and fighting to stand. Her wings sweep a gruesome pattern in the white. Her torso is concave. She scrabbles for her sword. I stamp on her hand and slice into her chest, her gargle swallowed by a howl of wind that cuts through my jacket and whips my hair across my face.

This is the way to kill angels—when they're half-mangled and immobile. Much easier, though my heart still slams against my ribs like it has wings of its own.

I charge around my Mitsubishi to help Hunter but he stands in a circle of broken bodies, splashes of silver bright on the white. His chest heaves. He flicks his wings and settles them against his back, the chalk holding up surprisingly well. I scan the sky, the flats, but nothing moves. Quiet drifts with the snowflakes. Hunter's shirt is ripped at the hem, dancing in the wind and giving glimpses of flat stomach and the line of his hip.

"What's your tally?" I say instead of throwing myself at him. He smirks. "Twenty."

"I guess you win again."

He closes the gap between us, not even looking at the bodies as he steps over them, his sword held away. He cups my face and I sink into the warmth of his hand.

"I win?" he says.

Snow sticks to his black hair and swirls in the darkness of his eyes.

"Always," I say and my voice only wobbles a little.

A smile teases his mouth. He bends that long body and his lips find mine. My knees melt. My sword slips from my hand and my fingers creep inside the rent of his shirt to stroke warm, silky skin.

An ache unfurls in my belly. An ache to be naked. Underneath him. Stretched and full and slave to the feel of him gliding in and out. All that muscle and power. All mine.

War and sex, indeed.

Metal clanks and Hunter eases me behind him but it's just our people, trickling from the buildings. Some are limping, skin streaked red, but every face holds a grin.

"You look flushed, Maia," Steph says, leaving track marks as she wheels forward.

She shares a smirk with Hunter and I roll my eyes, stepping out from the protective curve of his wing.

"Did we do it?" Greg shoves through the crowd, his eyes sparkling. His tinsel has come undone in the fight and his brown hair sticks to his cheeks. "Did we kill them all?"

"No," I say, and glance at Hunter. "No Persipha."

"No Persipha," he growls.

I pick up my bloodied sword and point it at the grey sky.

"To the castle!" I shout.

A cheer echoes in the avenue of fallen angels and snow.

30

Angel blood clots on my bonnet in lumps of grey. My gaze keeps darting to the stain as I forge a path through the virgin snow, a convoy of vehicles winding behind me, some struggling, tyres spinning on the slippery cobbles of the Royal Mile. My Mitsubishi purrs easily up the incline. The old buildings narrow at Castlehill then stop to leave the huge open space of the esplanade. Edinburgh Castle perches at the end, wreathed in white.

"It's beautiful," Steph breathes from the seat beside me.

She sits forward in her chair, hood thrown back, damp rainbow hair curled on her cheeks. Greg shoves his head between the seats, Mikey on one side of him and another Martello Court resident on the other. I offered Hunter a ride but he cocked his eyebrow, gave me a quick kiss and leapt into the sky.

If I had wings, I wouldn't want to get in a metal box, either.

"Shame it has a nest of vipers," Greg says.

Steph smirks. "Very poetic."

I motor onto the flat expanse and Edinburgh spreads below us to the north and south. The convoy follows, engines revving. We sweep down the esplanade like an invading army. A rampant lion crest is embedded in the wall above the arch of the gatehouse, the words *'Nemo me impune lacessit'* below it.

"'No one provokes me with impunity,'" Greg says.

I glance in the rearview mirror. "You speak Latin?"

"Hey, I read."

I ease to a stop. "Then let's go show them how provoked we are."

The convoy ranges in a semi-circle in front of the gatehouse. My fingers curl around the door handle.

Steph puts a hand on my arm. "Look."

Seven winged figures stand motionless on the battlements. A cape of auburn hair streams in the wind around the angel at the centre.

Persipha. The bitch.

"Seven," Mikey scoffs. "We can take seven."

Hunter appears on the battlements, casually settling his feathers. The angel on his right barely spares him a glance and receives an arrow to the temple. The next whips her head around and gets one in the eye. The third fires.

Hunter swoops off the battlements in a tight curve and draws his bowstring. Persipha sneers. His arrow flies for her cold, beautiful face. She cleaves it in two with a swipe of her glowing blue blade and launches towards him. He draws his sword and meets her, the clash of metal ringing through the car. Their swords blur. Feathers flare and flurry. They batter each other with wings and metal. Persipha swoops behind Hunter and he spins to face her. An angel on the battlements fires an arrow into his back. He flinches, losing height, but parries a vicious blow from Persipha.

"We need to get those bastards," I gasp.

We spill from the car, followed by everyone from the other vehicles. Arrows zip into the crowd. People charge for the gatehouse before I can open my mouth.

"Maia"—Steph winces and rubs her hip—"I don't think I can."

Greg looks at me, Mikey already sprinting through the archway, whooping and pumping his shield above his head as an arrow dings off.

"Stay with her," Greg says. "And him. We can get the rest."

"Good luck," I shout as he lopes away.

I usher Steph into the Mitsubishi. The clang-clang-clang of swords is constant. Persipha ducks, twists, dives, her slashing attacks unrelenting while I'm powerless, my throat closed in frustration and fear. The angels on the battlements strike Hunter twice more in the leg and shoulder before a roar of voices drags their attention behind them.

But the damage is done.

Persipha bats Hunter's blade to the side and kicks him in the gut. He sails backwards. Persipha nocks an arrow. Aims.

And shoots him in the chest.

"Hunter!" I scream.

His body thumps into the snow. My boots barely touch the ground. I suck air tasting of Hunter and it claws at my ribs. An arrow sings for my face. I yelp and jerk my shield up. The arrow rings off metal. My boots slide and I land on my arse, the impact juddering up my spine to my clenched jaw.

"Maia," Hunter groans, struggling to his knees, dazed black eyes on me.

Persipha fires an arrow into his stomach.

"Stop that, you fucking cow!" I screech.

I haul myself to my feet with the aid of my shield. Persipha sneers and says something to Hunter in their language. He barks at her and she laughs, tossing her shiny, auburn hair. She flings her bow to the ground and steps behind him. I start towards them. Hunter tries to grab her but she slaps his arms away. She catches his wing before he can shove her, wrenches it straight and breaks the bone between her hands. The snap vibrates deep in my stomach.

"Persipha," Hunter grunts, his eyes bright with pain, "you are a bitch."

She cocks her head. "What is a bitch?"

"*You,* you bitch," I snarl, and rush at her.

She kicks Hunter onto his face. Her sword sings from its sheath. Beautiful golden wings stretch wide to greet me.

I want to hack them to splinters.

Her blade howls in an arc and batters my shield. The blow jolts up my arm like an electric shock. I jab at one perfect, voluminous breast and she sweeps her sword into mine, wrenching it from my fingers.

Uh oh.

Her blade sings, crumpling my shield. I retreat, desperately clutching the metal, pain zinging up my arms. Each blow numbs my muscles.

I think of Hunter. How we met.

Persipha yanks the shield from my hands. Her feral grin freezes my boots to the snow, her eyes colder than the centre of a glacier. She towers over me. Her sword stays at her side, the horrible blue churning bile in my stomach. Scalding fingers wrap around my neck and squeeze. My boots leave the ground. I choke, and scrabble at her hand.

Hunter is a wavering ghost over her shoulder, lurching to his feet and staggering towards us, his broken wing drooping at an awkward angle.

Persipha says something in their musical language and tinkles a laugh. Hunter growls at her. Closer. *Closer.*

But he's going to be too late.

Her fingers gouge my skin, crushing my trachea in her palm.

She's not going to strangle me to death. She's going to rip out my throat.

She mocks Hunter. I memorise his face. His frantic expression. A hand curled around the arrow in his chest. Blood on his shirt.

"Hey, bitch," a voice snarls, "you picked a fight with the wrong universe."

I strain my eyes and there's Steph, leaning heavily on her cane, the door of the Mitsubishi gaping behind her. She flicks her dagger, just like she did when she first saw Hunter.

A pale mouth opens on Persipha's cheek. Silver blood spills and froths. Persipha howls and releases her hold on my neck. I crumple at her feet, dizziness threatening to smother me in white.

Or maybe it's the snow.

Blood throbs in my ears. My breath wheezes through my bruised throat.

"I will piss in your dust, *human*," Persipha says, a bloody hand clamped to her face.

She twirls her sword and steps over me. I grab two fistfuls of crimson hair and pull hard. Her heel catches my side. She tumbles onto her perfect arse, her palms braced on the ground to keep her from sprawling on her back. Her wings arch in fury.

"*You*," she hisses, glaring at me. "You, I will gut slowly."

She raises her sword and rolls to her knees. A black shape looms over her. An angel of death.

With a broken wing.

Hunter drags his blade across Persipha's throat.

31

Hot blood patters on my jacket and gums in my eyelashes, stinging my eyes. The chill of the snow seeps through my wet trousers and into my bones. I scrub my face with my gloves and blink at Hunter, back on his knees.

"Sorry," he says.

I scramble around Persipha's body, her head separated from the rest. Steph stays by the Mitsubishi, one hand on the door for balance, her cane uncertain on the slippery ground. My hands flutter over the arrows bristling from Hunter's torso.

"They cannot kill me," he says, breathing hard. "They just make me sick."

"Me, too."

I grab the shaft sticking from his chest. Ice zips to my shoulder and tingles in my teeth.

"Fast or slow?" I say, internalising a shudder.

Dark eyes meet mine. "Fast."

I yank the arrow. Blood daubs the tip, though none flows out to further stain his shirt thanks to his sealing ability. Pain glazes his eyes but he stays silent. I tug the rest quickly, bile squirting into my throat. My sword splinters the shafts and the blue light fades, though the nausea remains. I leave Persipha's sword untouched, the malevolent glow softly smothered by the snow. I wrap my arms around the solidness of Hunter, both of us on our knees, and bury my nose in his neck.

"I will be okay," he murmurs in my ear, "but I will need sleep soon."

"What about your wing?"

"You will have to pull the bone straight so it does not heal crooked and need re-broken."

I shiver, and his arms tighten around me.

"How many times have your wings been broken?"

"Too many to count."

I slot myself under his shoulder and help him to his feet. We limp across to Steph.

"Greg says they're cornering the last one." She clutches the radio in the hand resting on the door. "Mikey got dusted."

I shake my head. "How many more?"

"A few. He says they have light and heat inside."

"The castle has solar?"

"Creator technology," Hunter says, his voice strained. "No pollution."

"Couldn't they have given us that rather than angels of death?"

He shrugs the shoulder I'm tucked under. "They believe punishment is the only way to learn."

"Righteous bastards," I say. "But I guess I wouldn't have met you if they'd chosen aid over war."

He slides me an implacable Hunter look. "Was it worth it?"

"Yes," I say, and he gives me a shy smile.

"You two are so cute," Steph sighs. "The savage warrior angel tamed by the tiny, gentle human."

"I'll give you tiny," I grumble.

Hunter tilts my chin with his finger. "You are gentle with

me."

My lips find his, tasting ice and something citrusy. Probably Persipha's blood but I don't stop kissing him. Steph sighs some more.

I pull away and suck in a cold breath to steady myself. "Let's patch you up in the castle. I could do with some heat."

Hunter allows Steph to support him—a massive show of trust given his aversion to people touching him—and I grab her wheelchair from the back of the Mitsubishi. She offers it to Hunter but he just stares at her. She raises her hands and settles into the chair, her cane collapsed and in her lap. She wheels a path through the snow while I steer a limping Hunter.

"I wonder how everyone else got on," she says.

"If they don't kill enough, we'll have to leave the city. Widen the hunt."

She shudders. "Then I hope they kill enough."

The hacked and bubbling corpse of an angel decorates the floor of the gatehouse. A white-gold feather sticks to a splash of blood on the stone.

"This is a bit beyond getting a lump of coal for being bad," Steph says grimly.

I snort. Hunter sags against me, his eyes half-lidded.

"Is he going to be okay?" She waits for me at the foot of the curving road leading up to the next gate.

"Healing takes a lot of energy. He'll probably pass out soon."

"I will not pass out," Hunter says.

Steph smirks. "He's as stubborn as you."

Snow peppers a lion rampant crest above a second gate, a black portcullis set in the thick stone arch. We enter the winter wonderland of the castle proper. Wind howls around ancient walls and cannons. Two black metal bollards guide us under another rough stone arch. Excited voices bounce around a wide square flanked on all sides by stone buildings, one with a tall tower, clock face and mullioned windows. Greg jogs across, silver blood clotted in his hair.

"I'm sorry about Mikey," I say.

He nods and examines the grey sky, his eyes shiny.

"Thanks," he says gruffly. "Is your angel okay?"

"He just needs to rest. Are there any beds in this place?"

"Second floor of the Royal Palace." He nods at the building with the tower. "You'll have to go through the Laich Hall. Sorry about the mess."

"The what hall?"

Greg manages a lip twitch. "You need to read more, Maia."

Our rag-tag army circles us, noticeably smaller in number than when we started out. Hunter curls his uninjured wing around me and watches them through black, hooded eyes.

"What now, Boss?" Steph smirks, snowflakes in her rainbow hair.

I glare at her then raise my chin.

"If this place has light and heat, let's hole up here. Greg—take a group with 4x4s and round up supplies before the snow really comes in." I toss him my car keys. "Steph—grab a few people and find bandages and something I can use as a splint. The rest of you—set up a watch in pairs for tonight in case we missed any angels."

There, that all sounds commanding.

"Aye-aye, Captain," Steph says, saluting and wheeling away with a bunch of Martello Court residents.

The others disperse without a grumble and I hide my incredulous expression.

"You are a good leader," Hunter says, sagging a little more

now that we're alone.

"I don't know what the hell I'm doing."

"Maybe you *are* built for war."

I shudder. "I hope this is the last war I ever see."

The mess in the Laich Hall turns out to be a dismembered angel, bloody limbs scattered in piles of dust. A head has rolled into the empty fireplace. Hunter and I leave boot prints in the carnage.

I hoist him up a narrow, winding staircase to a second floor of stately rooms and lower him onto a huge four-poster bed, the canopy trimmed in red and gold. A thick carpet muffles my steps. The mullioned windows look out onto the empty square, tracks in the snow spreading in all directions. A radiator puffs heat against my damp jeans and I want to hug it.

"Maia," Hunter mumbles, his face buried in the brocade covers. "You have to fix my wing."

"Can't I wait until you're unconscious?"

"No."

I huff out a breath. "I don't want to hurt you."

"It will hurt me more if it needs re-broken."

"How will I know if I'm doing it right? What if I make it worse?"

He quirks his mouth while I wring my hands and pace.

"I trust you," he says.

"Goddammit," I sigh. "Tell me what to do."

I approach the bed warily and he watches me out of one eye, half of his face buried in the covers. His blue shirt is soaked and moulded to his back, his trousers and boots unmarred and seemingly indestructible.

"Hold above the first joint," he says. "Straighten the wing. You will feel the bones slot together at the break."

I grit my teeth to keep them from chattering. Soft feathers tickle my palms, dusty from the chalk. His wing flops at the broken humerus. Hunter turns his head to watch me. Steady, even pressure straightens his wing. The fractured bone shifts. His flinch is almost imperceptible but I've been studying his expressions for weeks now. I hesitate.

"Keep going," he says.

My stomach rolls but I straighten his wing. Bones scrape. Something cracks and clicks under my fingertips. Hunter's wing flops but no longer at an unnatural angle near his back. His whole body seems to melt.

"Now I will pass out," he says, and passes out.

32

"Have you done this before?"

Steph holds our makeshift splint on the underside of Hunter's wing. The two metal poles lie parallel to his broken humerus and stick out beyond the first joint and where his wing meets his shoulder. Cotton padding hides the shape. I tape a strip of bandage to the end of the splint and gently fold Hunter's wing into a normal position against his back.

"I saw my mum do it once," I say. "To a bird."

Steph smirks. "Oh, just the same thing then."

"I'm trying to think of him as a really big magpie."

Steph laughs, keeping the wing and splint in place. Hunter breathes quietly, his lashes black against his cheekbones. I roll the bandage over the bend of his wing and under the outer edge towards his body, wrapping it in a figure of eight.

"He may be black and somewhat white but no magpie has an arse like that."

"Stop checking out my boyfriend's arse."

I'm surprised he hasn't startled awake as soon as we manipulated his wing. Maybe it's too soon in the healing process, unlike when I stepped on him in Newhailes after he'd been sliced and diced.

I loop figures of eight with the bandage until the splint is secure.

"Okay, now I need you to hold him up so I can wrap this around his chest."

We shuffle across the bed. Steph stands between his legs, wobbling on the springy mattress, and slides her hands into his armpits.

"Wow, he's hot, isn't he?"

"Steph, for god's sake..."

"I mean his skin, Maia." She shoots me another smirk. "Though he is pretty hot."

She lifts his torso off the bed and sneezes when his feathers tickle her nose. I roll the tape under his chest, arm and uninjured wing then across his broken wing and back again a couple of times. Steph lowers him to the bed and sits hard beside me, bouncing a little.

"You know, this is the first time we've been alone since you started being nice to your indestructible angel boyfriend."

I nod at the sleeping Hunter. "We're hardly alone. And he's semi-indestructible."

"He's in no position to listen." She leans close. "What's he like in bed?"

"Technically, I've never had sex with him in a bed."

"Come on, Maia, I'm dying here. I need details—dirty, sexy details. He looks like he could make a girl forget her own name."

I crawl off the bed to hide my pink cheeks, and Steph follows. I spread the duvet over Hunter and sit by the radiator, Steph sinking into her wheelchair.

"He's"—I glance at the lump under the covers and lower my voice—"fucking awesome."

Steph grins. "Built like that, he just has to be. God, I'm so jealous."

"And he's"—another peek at Hunter—"*huge*. I mean, scary huge but he never hurts me. He does, however, leave me unable to walk for a while."

Steph slaps my arm. "I hate you, you lucky cow."

I hug my legs to my chest and rest my cheek on my knees, watching Hunter sleep, only his dark head visible on the pillow. He could be comatose for days but I miss him already. Miss his intense, midnight-blue gaze. His unguarded smile. His curiosity. The way he cocks his head. The touch of his hands, cradling me like I'm fragile.

Which I am, compared to him.

"You should introduce him to your dad, he'll have a fit. When this is all over, obviously, and if your dad is... You know."

I drag my eyes to Steph.

"I guess it also depends if he still believes in the 'Holy Angels.'" I make air quotes with my fingers. "Though I bet he does. He'll say God sent them to test our faith. But a reconciliation might be worth it for his reaction. And there's nothing like the apocalypse to make you want to reconnect with family."

"Well, he can't say you're not a good Catholic girl now."

"Oh, he might if he ever finds out what that angel does to me."

We giggle like a couple of teenagers instead of two soldiers in humanity's last army. A knock at the door disturbs us and I climb to my feet. Greg stands in the corridor, his cheeks pink from the cold.

"Hey, Maia. We're going to have dinner in the Great Hall in about thirty minutes but there's something you should see. We think it's where the angels were staying when they were here. It's creepy, man."

I glance over my shoulder at the bed.

I can't leave Hunter alone when he's unconscious and vulnerable.

"I'll watch him," Steph says, wheeling across the thick carpet. "He's in safe hands."

"As long as you keep those hands to yourself."

She wiggles her fingers at me. "Promise."

She's definitely going to poke him.

I close the door behind me and trail Greg down the stairs into the Laich Hall. Three people from Martello Court are scrubbing the blood off the walls and floor, the remains of the angel gone.

"We're burning their bodies on the Argyle Battery," Greg says to my unasked question. "This castle is a symbol of Edinburgh. Of Scotland. We're not having it covered in their guts."

"We'll need a pretty big fire at Muirhouse."

Greg grins. "We'll get to that, though I'd happily stay in the castle til the world has power again."

He leads me into a huge room with an open timber ceiling and bright-red walls. Chandeliers twinkle on long chains. People bustle around, setting up tables and chairs. Through a door in the far corner, a staircase leads down into darkness.

"There are lights in the vaults," Greg says to my hesitation.

My boots slap stone. The blackness brightens to yellow in a cavernous room. Something blue shimmers on the far wall and my hand tightens on my sword. Greg strides towards it. Barred cells contain raised concrete platforms and arched lintels. The air smells of damp stone.

"It's not exactly a cosy base of operations is it—even for warrior angels?" My voice and our footsteps echo.

"And they left no trace of themselves. Except for this." Greg nods at the shimmering blue.

A string of digits seems to float on the brick wall, the same exact colour as their swirly soulreaver arrows and swords.

"Is that what I think it is?" I breathe.

"Yup," Greg says grimly. "Their global tally."

The blue number ripples on the wall and my stomach rolls. Not because it'll suck my soul to dust if I touch it. But because of how high it is.

The digits read 3,783,773,112.

"Jesus," I whisper. "They're not far off their target. They might bloody win after all."

Greg shakes his head. "When we first found it, the number flicked up a couple of digits but it's not changed since then."

"So no one else is dying?"

"Nope." Greg bares his teeth. "But I hope those fuckers are."

* * *

A fidgeting Hunter startles me from a dream featuring him tied to a bed and me on top.

Hunter never fidgets. He's like a giant man-brick when he falls asleep.

He throws the covers off and sits on the edge of the bed, his silhouette framed in the lighter blackness of the windows. Snow taps on the glass.

"Go," he says.

I knuckle the sleep from my eyes. "Go where? What are you talking about?"

"It is time to go."

His voice isn't right. Robotic almost.

My heart kicks and I reach for the lamp on the bedside

cabinet. Light floods the room, casting colours on the bed canopy through the glass of the shade.

It's Tiffany, according to Steph. Very expensive.

Hunter doesn't react to the light, his back to me. One wing stretches out, off-white and chalky. His broken wing twitches but the bandage holds.

"Hunter?" I place a hand on his warm skin.

He jumps to his feet and pivots neatly on his heel. There's nothing familiar in his face. His eyes are black and empty and terrifying.

He reaches behind his shoulder, his fingers clasping air, as if searching for a bow. Or a sword. My heart freezes and drops into my stomach. He shakes his head and strides for the door.

"Wait," I yelp, scrambling from the bed before my brain can tell me it's a bad idea to accost a warrior angel.

His hand twists the brass knob. A slice of harsh white light dazzles my retinas. I slide my body between Hunter and the door. The wood bumps closed. I place my palms on his solid chest.

"Hunter, look at me."

Goosebumps flare when his dark gaze meets mine. I stretch on tippy-toe, and pray.

My lips find his. I slip my hands into his hair and press myself against him, tensed for fingers to crush my biceps and rip me away. He shudders. Hands cup my back.

Oh, god, he's going to tear my spine out in his fist.

"Maia?" he whispers against my lips.

"Oh, thank Christ," I gasp, and sag in his arms. "You weren't *you* for a second there."

He eases me away, his hands on my shoulders, scanning me from head to toe, his eyes panicked.

"Did I hurt?"

I trace his mouth. "You'd never hurt me."

He hugs me to his chest, his heart thudding in my ear. "It was our creators. They have ordered the retreat."

I snuggle into his comforting scent of ice plus a hint of chalk. He eases me away again with a soft smile.

"We did it, Maia," he says. "We did it."

33

One Year Later

My slightly shaking finger reaches for the doorbell and presses the round button. *Amazing Grace* chimes through the tidy, terraced house.

My childhood home.

The bare branches of the cherry tree in the front garden scrape in the wind and I pat at my hair for the twentieth time since we got off the train at Armadale.

"You do not have to do this," Hunter says beside me, dressed in his customary black and looking good enough to unwrap and eat.

But now is probably not the best time.

He acquiesced to getting on the train rather than flying above it, though he kept me in the protective circle of his arms, his wings flaring if anyone approached. Not many did. They pointed their phones at us and whispered in excited voices instead.

He's still intimidating even though he no longer carries a bow and arrows or a sword. He refuses to get rid of his knives, though.

"It's fine," I say, and squeeze his hand. "I want to do this."

A shape appears behind the glass of the front door. I grip Hunter's hand harder and he smirks at me. A chain scrapes. A lock clicks. The door swings inward. My dad's mouth gapes and he falls to his knees.

Okay, so maybe it was a bit petty not to tell him my boyfriend was a warrior angel.

For the last few months, we've had careful, excruciatingly polite phone calls in negotiation for this meeting. What to say, what not to say. What behaviour will make a certain prodigal daughter leave and never come back.

"Maia!" my dad says with only the barest of hitches. "Your boyfriend is a Holy Angel! The holiest of Holy Angels!"

I was bang on target with how my dad interpreted the apocalypse. He set up the Order of the Holy Angels and eschewed all modern contrivances for a simpler, cleaner life. They considered it the highest honour to be dusted by an angel, their bodies nourishing the world they left behind. They went out and prayed in the streets. It's a wonder he's still alive, though his congregation rapidly decreased. Their numbers have certainly swelled over the last year.

Thankfully, Hunter is not the only Holy Angel for them to fawn over.

"Hi... Dad," I say with my own hitch.

He climbs to his feet, wearing an undyed tunic and loose trousers the colour of porridge. Sparse grey hair wisps from the top of his head.

He looks older than I remember. Thinner.

He waves at us. "Come in, come in, Maia, Your Excellency. Can I call you Your Excellency?"

"His name is Hunter," I say with nary an eye roll.

Hunter holds out his hand, well-versed in human social customs now. He gives my dad his arrogant face and intense blue-black eyes. Dad practically vibrates when their palms touch.

The living room is almost exactly as I left it eleven years ago—sagging blue couch, Mum's favourite armchair covered by a plaid throw, her picture on the mantelpiece next to the ancient Zenith radio. The only thing missing is the TV.

Dad shoos us onto the sofa. "Tea? Coffee?"

"Tea, please," I say, sitting primly, knees together.

My jeans and maroon hoodie are the most conservative clothes I own. My t-shirts all have funny slogans my dad probably wouldn't get.

I've purchased racier things recently. Mostly underwear. Hunter loves to take it off. With his teeth.

I shiver and Hunter glances at me. The clink of ceramic comes from the direction of the kitchen.

After he told me about the Creator's call to retreat—humanity one, warrior angels zero—he slipped back into his healing coma for three days. Then he woke up and looked at me with dark, hungry eyes and I got to wash his wings like he'd promised. The shower was huge. Tiled grey and blue. Hunter stood under the stream, water spiking his hair and beading in his lashes. Chalk swirled down the drain. My greedy hands moved to slick, hot skin. He pinned me to the cold tile and took his sweet, glorious time, my legs wrapped around his waist, his—

"What are you thinking, Maia?" Hunter says, his voice doing the soft, growly thing that pools heat in low places.

Oh, crap. I'm stroking his thigh.

I clear my throat. "I'm thinking I'd quite like to get you home soon."

He grins at me and captures my hand, pressing it to the laces of his trousers and the huge, hard length of him beneath.

"I would like that, too," he says.

"Oat milk and sugar?" my dad says, and I whip my hands into my lap.

Dad places a tray on the coffee table, steam purling from the spout of the teapot. An unfamiliar hymn plays on the radio.

The power was restored about eight months ago, apart from the periodic, planned blackouts since we're only using renewable energy until the Creator's technology has been mass-produced. Fossil fuels were banned without a whimper of protest, though there wasn't much left of the workforce of the oil and gas giants.

No one wants another lesson in green energy from the Creators.

It also helped that the angels dusted most of the United States and Saudi Arabia.

"Three sugars for Hunter, one for me and we'll both have milk," I say.

Hunter discovered the delights of human food and has a sweet tooth. It's so cute.

Dad hands us each a delicate china cup. Hunter cradles it carefully in his hands and I hide a smile. Dad takes his tea milky and perches in Mum's chair.

"Have you given any thought to moving to a bigger house?" Dad's eyes flick towards Hunter's wings arching above his shoulders. "It must be quite cramped in your flat."

As nice as it would've been to live in Edinburgh Castle forever, we bequeathed it back to what remained of the Scottish Government.

"I love Martello Court," I say. "We all fought together. The community is amazing."

Living in a flat keeps the gawkers away and Hunter can easily come and go from the balcony. Steph also has a new roommate.

But I miss Newhailes sometimes. The National Trust for Scotland says we can visit anytime. They've recreated a shrine of our room for tourists to marvel over.

"And your friend—Stephanie—she still lives there?"

"She does. She actually has her own warrior angel boyfriend."

Dad's eyes light up. "You should bring them round for a visit. You and-and Hunter. Are you in touch with the other Holy Angels?"

"We talk," I say.

They arrived, unarmed, on our fifth day in the castle—a troop of twenty angels with wings the colour of gemstones. They'd chosen to ignore the Creator's call, the same as Hunter. I'll never forget the astonishment on his face.

He wasn't the only one who wanted to be gentle.

Steph walked right up to a male with blond hair to his shoulders and sapphire eyes that matched his wings, and introduced herself. Greg looked crestfallen and Devinon never stood a chance. I had to have the stern talk about not hurting her after only a day. Now, Devinon carries her around with the most besotted look on his face. I've never seen Steph so happy.

We were both unhappy for enough of last year when the recovering government decided the angels should be contained and studied. It was a struggle to get Hunter and the rest freed, even with the hundreds of voices raised in support. The Scottish Government finally let them out when they promised to help set the world to rights and share the secrets of Creator technology.

"Do you think they would agree to address my congregation?" Dad says, practically bouncing in his chair. "And Hunter? I can't tell you how ecstatic they'd be to worship the Holy Angels in person."

"No," Hunter says, and sips his tea.

I give him an encouraging eyebrow arch.

"Though I do not speak for the others," he says.

Dad pumps the air, spilling tea onto his leg but he doesn't appear to notice.

"Wonderful! Oh, that would be wonderful if you could put in a good word with the other Holy Angels." Dad glances at me, his cheeks flushed. "You should see our church, Maia. It would be a beautiful location for your wedding."

I choke on my tea. "My what now?"

"Your wedding to Hunter. Surely you are planning a wedding?"

"Jeez, Dad, it's only been a year."

Something fluttery happens in my chest. I try not to look at Hunter but I can't seem to help it.

Hunter cocks his head. "What is a wedding?"

Oh, *Christ*.

I'm going to have a semi-indestructible angel husband.

Let Me Know What You Think!

Thank you for reading my book! I love hearing from my readers so please leave me a review.

Can't wait to hear from you!

For awesome bonus content, including a free prequel to my Scottish dystopian series, join my mailing list at nadinelittle.com/free-prequel by scanning the QR code below:

Watch Out for the Next Book in the Series:
We Are Not Broken
The Creators are not done with Maia and Hunter.
Far from it.

About the Author

Nadine Little lives in Scotland and is an ecologist who loves botany. This may be one of her few books without anything resembling a dragon. The story came about when she'd reached a snag in her novel *Verdana* and had no idea how it was going to end. As a break, she decided to write about the soothing topics of global catastrophe and surviving an angel apocalypse.

You're welcome.

For more on her books and a peek into her general weirdness, sign up to her mailing list and follow her on social media.

You can connect with me on:
- https://nadinelittle.com
- https://twitter.com/Nadine_Little_
- https://www.facebook.com/nadinelittleauthor

Subscribe to my newsletter:
- https://nadinelittle.com/free-prequel

CPSIA information can be obtained
at www.ICGtesting.com
Printed in the USA
BVHW040925061222
653555BV00005B/92